Ghosts and More...

tales of the supernatural:
an anthology

John Hanford, Chuck Hocter, R.M. Kinder,
James Henry Taylor, Chanda K. Zimmerman

LiquidAmber Publishing
Henderson, Nevada

9 8 7 6 5 4 3 2 1

*Ghosts and More . . . tales of the supernatural:
an anthology*

ISBN-13: 978-0-9895034-5-7 (print)
978-0-9895034-6-4 (e-book)

Cover photo by Peter H. (Tama66) :
https://pixabay.com/photos/pforphoto-library-left-
house-6578797/

Special thanks to
the Blackwater Literary Society, founded in 1996,
Warrensburg, Missouri.

FOREWORD

There are many reasons writers pool their talents to create a collection, and this one includes one of the most popular subjects in both fiction and non-fiction—ghosts. The Blackwater Society, a local writers' critique group, of which I'm proud to have been a member, has created hauntingly unique stories that mix fantasy, horror, and magical realism into a tightly woven compilation.

John Hanford's pieces have a skin of hope but with a more sinister underbelly. Just when you think you know where the tale is going, there is a punchy twist at the end to make you rethink preconceived notions.

Chuck Hocter creates stories through observations, crafting tales that leave you wondering if every creak and groan of your house is a spirit seeking to communicate.

R.M. Kinder's stories have an innate sense of longing and release that drives the narrative as she examines the idea that ghosts can bring comfort to a lonely heart. I am a fan of her lush flair for language! Her languid writing style takes you on almost dream-like journeys.

James Henry Taylor can turn a slice of life story into something edgy, distinctive, and unsettling. From unwanted visitors to gambling with the supernatural, he proves that not even the devil is safe from his machinations.

Chanda K. Zimmerman's sense of whimsy treats the afterlife as another adventure. Whether human or animal, death is just the beginning for her ghosts.

These condensed tales explore a multitude of possibilities when it comes to spirits. Whether it's a grizzled veteran waiting to tell his story, a woman who's willing to leave the living behind to keep the dead, a warning from an ancestor that saves a soldier's life, a cat who ferries the spirits of those it loves, or a child experiencing the loss of a not-so imaginary friend, and more, these characters and their stories stay with you long after you've finished reading them.

Do you believe in ghosts? I'm not sure I do, but this collection makes me want to consider the possibilities.

—Renee George, *USA Today* Bestselling Author of the **Nora Black Midlife Psychic Mysteries**

Stories

Sleepover by Chuck Hocter 7

Eternity Can Wait by Chanda K. Zimmerman   11

Moving On by John Hanford 37

Visitings by James Henry Taylor 57

Loving Ghosts by R.M. Kinder 63

FIN by Chuck Hocter 87

The Unkindest Cut by James Henry Taylor ... 95

A Life Denied by John Hanford 115

The Fourth Floor by R.M. Kinder 131

Seeing Is Believing by Chanda K. Zimmerman   149

The Tunnel by Chuck Hocter 165

The Boy with No Name by John Hanford 189

Bringing Them Home by R.M. Kinder 205

Margie and Sadie by James Henry Taylor 209

Night Guardian by Chanda K. Zimmerman ... 217

Sleepover
by Chuck Hocter

The yawn stretched her clear down to her toes, a sure sign that it was way past time for her to call it a night. As she started down the hallway to the bathroom, she could hear the boys trying to muffle their roughhousing and laughter. Sleepovers, she thought, gotta love 'em.

"All right, guys, time for bed. Fun's over for tonight."

Immediate silence in her son's bedroom was soon followed by a plaintive, "Aw Mom, just a few minutes more. Please?"

She was tempted to spoil him a little but another tremendous yawn reminded her that she had to be up early and the two boys had school. "Sorry, not tonight. Maybe next time we can do this on a weekend and stay up all night. Okay?"

From behind the closed door came a grudging agreement. "Okay. Goodnight, Mom."

"Goodnight, boys. Sleep tight and don't let the ghoulies bite."

She was about to enter the bathroom when she realized that the kitchen light was still on though she distinctly remembered turning it off. As she headed back down the hallway, she smiled. Just our invisible housemate, she thought. Ever since they had moved in, there had been a series of small, insignificant incidents such as misplaced items, cold spots, lights being left on, etc. Nothing scary or dangerous—just curious and usually accompanied by the faint smell of lilac, a scent not used by any of the occupants of the house.

Sure enough, as she flipped the switch, darkening the kitchen, the familiar odor filled the air, stronger than usual. "Good night, old friend. Have a peaceful evening." Her whisper hung in the air for just a second, a chill running up her spine. She shook it off and returned to her nightly bedtime routine.

She came awake suddenly. Something familiar yet frightening had disturbed her sleep. It was the sound of her husband's combat boots as if he were walking down the hallway coming to bed. The problem was, he was halfway round the world, deployed with his unit. She could feel the hairs on her arms starting to come to attention when it dawned on her that it must be the boys, fooling around and trying to frighten her. She got up, put on her robe and was almost to the door of her bedroom, ready to put the fear of God into a couple of young hooligans, when from the vicinity of the kitchen came a horrendous crash and shattering of glass. She flung open the door to reveal two terrified youngsters who grabbed her in a double bear hug.

"Mom, what's happening?"

"What have you two done?"

"We didn't do anything, I swear!"

Their terror seemed to be entirely genuine. "You two stay here. I'll go see what's going on." She flipped on the hallway light but couldn't see anything out of the ordinary. She entered the kitchen, expecting to see glass shards everywhere but the light revealed none at all. When she had heard the shattering glass earlier, her first thought had been that the boys had been fooling around and had knocked an ancient and precious glass pitcher off of the top of the refrigerator. But there it was in its familiar perch, all in one piece. Something strange about the handle of the pitcher caught her eye. She took it down and gave it a close inspection. To her amazement, the glass of the handle—in fact of the whole pitcher—appeared to have been shattered then seamlessly repaired, piece fitted to piece so perfectly that the surface was completely smooth.

She took the pitcher to the table, set it down, pulled up a chair and sat. As she contemplated this impossible situation, memories of all the other unusual incidents came back to her. They had all been harmless, even funny. They had never been frightening or violent—until now. Had their invisible housemate somehow changed? Her thoughts were interrupted by a wafting of the fragrance of lilac—with just the hint of sulfur and brimstone.

Author Comments:

This is based on true events which took place while I was deployed. Those involved were my wife, my son, his friend, and a terrified Great Pyrenees named Butter Paws Brookes. I did take a bit of poetic license. No one reported a smell of brimstone.

Eternity Can Wait
by Chanda K. Zimmerman

So I am dead. Must be. I don't remember much, except waking up in the hospital, briefly, and then waking up again and looking down on myself with a mixture of affection, pity, and a curious lack of concern about the whole thing. I saw them working to help me, save me—*save* me, hm, heard that one before in church in a rather different perspective. Well, I must say, this is not what I expected of the Pearly Gates. I thought things would be more … *heavenly.* As in, I wouldn't be standing here in the public library. Standing here? Floating? Existing? *Not existing?*

I didn't start out here. First, to no one's surprise, I am sure, I went home to check on the cats since I live—lived—alone. They were a bit freaked out. Cats can see things a lot of humans can't. Some of them were more curious than others, some totally bored because I didn't have food, and others fleeing to hide under the yellow chair. Poor things. But they understood and I assured them that I would make certain that someone came. The two strays took it better than the indoor cats.

Thankfully, my dear friends and family, and eventually blood family living far away, rallied. They followed the protocols I had laid out in my incredibly detailed instructions (Bless

Paige's heart: she was right on top of everything despite all her own obligations). After a few days—was it days or weeks?—of people coming in and caring for them, they got the cats into the kennel for a brief stint, and then they went on to new homes, some with family, some with friends, some to a decent, kindly shelter. I checked on every one of them, unnoticed of course.

And after that, people came and began to clean out the house, removing the photos of my parents and the painting of my grandmother, and all the things that used to mean so much to me. I thought I couldn't part with them, but I felt a curious detachment … as if they had belonged to someone else. With everything gone, there really wasn't any real reason to stay. My writing, the only thing that mattered to me otherwise, was, alas, for the most part not going to ever see the light of publication, except for a few short pieces published by friends before and after. I saw that Paige understood the needs of the two stray cats and somehow they were rescued. Nothing more needed to happen. Well, such was life. Or, to be more precise, such was death.

So I moved out of the old house—heavens, I didn't want to haunt some poor family that thought they'd bought the home of their dreams. I didn't have anything to get vengeance over. I wandered the neighborhood at night, following the little creatures flitting through my backyard like little ghosts in the shadows, foraging for food. The foxes were fast, the raccoons erratic, the cats for the most part seemed to be owned and indoors although I saw a few strays who had their supporters in other parts of the subdivision. But after a while, even that became rather a bore.

I kept wondering where the hell heaven was—if you'll

pardon my "French." But even hell wasn't any more obvious to me than the other side. And the one thing I really had hated to think about during my life—coming back here in some other form—didn't seem to be an option either. I mean there was no neon sign, blinking "Get your reincarnation here!" Nor would I have applied. When I was young, it had seemed rather attractive, but after this many years and way too much experience, I really wasn't sure I wanted it. In fact, I was pretty sure I didn't. This world, this "vale of tears" and hardness, cruelty and kindness, so frustrating in its potential, so filled with problems that never got solved and never should have existed … well, why would I look forward to that all over again?

The only thing I had come to hope for after death was some rest. I just wanted to lie down and forget it all: no more bills I didn't know how to pay, no people telling me what was wrong with me, and giving me endless lectures about how to do better, chiding me for being too emotional, and trying to "fix" me—as if I were some sort of a DIY project that they needed to be completed for them to get into heaven. I understood that most of them meant well, although at times it got damned tedious and I was ready to chuck it all. I knew all of them were actually just as confused themselves. However, I would have preferred they focus their "home improvement" obsession on someone besides me—like their own lives.

Anyway, I eventually in my wanderings rediscovered the public library, and decided to stay for a while. Nice and quiet most of the time. But during business hours, it was particularly satisfying and enjoyable to watch the people of all ages and persuasions coming and going, immersed in books, videos, and activities that the library put on. The meetings were a hoot. Some public, some private, some ridiculously self-righteous, some overly serious, others a bit wayward and not well organized—but all *soooo* earnest. Little did they know, it really wouldn't matter one jot after … well, afterward.

I think my favorites were the Halloween events, like the lecture on ghost hunting, presented by an earnest group of "experts." That made me smile. Talk about expert. I could give them a tip or two. The meeting was a big do, replete with cookies and punch, and attended by a fairly large bunch of people who desperately wanted to encounter a ghost. Ah, if only they knew … I suspect most were desperately hoping there was something after death, although some hid it by presenting themselves as hardened skeptics. What, I wondered, were they doing here then if it was all just a delusion of some kind?

I stood in the back during the lecture, watching the presenters—a sixty-seven-year-old founder of a local paranormal group, his wife, and a couple of their 20-something proteges. During the break, standing behind the little groups of attendees talking about their experiences, I started wondering if I dared try nibbling a chocolate chip cookie, the only thing that had appealed to me after my "demise"—although once or twice the smell of good coffee down at the bakery sent a momentary and well-remembered pang of desire through me.

As I stood watching these people, all warm flesh and blood, pulses and hearts pounding, eyes bright and cheeks flushed with excitement, I found myself wondering what the effect would be if I just blew in someone's ear or ran a finger across their shoulders. Would they even know? I hadn't really developed an expertise at doing things physically, but I had tried my hand at knocking some books off shelves. The first one or two were rather exciting, but as I began to get the hang of it—just enough to irritate one of the older librarians pushing a cart to restock the shelves—it was just another boring thing. But this, finding a way to interact, to give someone hoping for something spooky a tiny little thrill…

But I didn't. I really did not want to be the cause of a heart attack—and I certainly did not want to have to deal with the emotional (and eternal) fallout of a moment's thoughtless whim if that person ended up roving the library like so many of us did. More to the point, I suspected that none of these would-be ghost hunters actually wanted to join the "fun" as a new card-carrying member of the dearly departed.

So, at the moment, I was on my best behavior, standing next to Margie, an older woman like myself who, not having any family to haunt, often hung out at the library, although she also spent a good deal of time at her church—the big United Methodist one with the front doors that looked like one was entering the Roman Senate. Sometimes her little scruffy brown dog, Jasper, who preceded her by a couple of years into the afterlife, joins us, although he seems to spend most of his time elsewhere. Anyway, I said to Margie that I thought the information was intriguing and that we should accompany them sometime on one of their ghost-hunting adventures. Margie yawned and said she really didn't want to run into one of those nasty ghosts they're always showing on the videos and TV shows. She also thought it would be a bit of "cheating"—sort of a "bring your own ghost" event more than an investigation. She had a point, I had to admit. Sort of took all the sport out of it.

Matthew, a good-looking young man, almost 30 (or he had been before his fatal motorcycle incident some years back), with long, dark, curly hair hanging past his shoulders, was eyeing the cookies, too. Seriously, I loved those long dark curls: if I'd been 30 years younger myself… I sighed and surveyed the happy crowd until I heard a soft "Boo!" in my ear. I jumped a foot until, as usual, I remembered I was a ghost, too.

"Honestly, Matthew, that trick is getting pretty old," I chided.

He chuckled. "Still made you jump, though!"

Margie shook her head, looking at the assortment of folk who had turned out for the event. "I don't know why all these people want to go looking for ghosts. Look at that, those children! Don't their parents have any sense? Bringing a child to something like this, talking about spooks and hauntings… Really!"

"Oh, it's just good fun, Marg." Matthew smiled at her glare. She hated it when he called her Marg. "They don't really run into anything too bad, at least not this group."

"And how would you know?"

"Well," he looked down with a grin and back up at her in challenge, "I tagged along once on one of their adventures." Matthew shrugged. "Didn't find much—just a few unidentified wisps of smoke or fog, some fuzzy orbs, and the usual occasional disembodied word caught on tape, hard to tell from interference on the radio."

"Where?"

"Old place down on south 13, just before that big curve. Geez, that was a great ride on the bike…" he mused, lost in a past moment. I knew the old house. It was reputed to be haunted. It had always looked haunted to me, on my drives down to Clinton, as if it had been built not long after the Civil War. But for the life of me, I had no idea why any ghost would want to live in its bedraggled state even in the afterlife. The place looked ready to crumble in the next big storm—had looked that way for more than a decade.

"Only ghosts I saw were the little guys, you know, like the mice and insects, along with a respectable number of their very much alive cousins." Matthew smiled wistfully. "Had a nice chat with a dead lizard and a live owl, but beyond that it was a little boring. Those guys need a little more practice or something." He indicated the paranormal team all standing beside their fearless leader at the front of the meeting room, staring rapt at the screen with shots of one of the city graveyards, a corner set aside for Civil War veterans. "After six or eight hours in that old wreck, even I was disappointed when they gave up the 'ghost' so to speak, and the team went home without anything. In fact, the whole thing was rather a depressing bore, so I hightailed it down to the cowboy bar."

I knew which one he meant. A "meat market" in the old terms, where college kids hung out getting plastered, indulging in what passed for dancing these days, and looking for love in all the wrong places. But I knew also that Matthew found some measure of peace with his current existence by remaining outside the bar, and monitoring the patrons who were departing. He had confessed to me that he liked to intervene if they were about to do something they'd regret, as he had one night, taking a difficult curve too fast on his motorcycle after a lethal combo of drinks and drugs. His intervention of choice was usually just to do something to their starter to keep the engine from cranking. One night, he returned to the library in exceptionally high spirits (my goodness, I made a pun!) and all I could get out of him was that he'd given a couple of bullies a few white hairs and sent them fleeing from the dimly lit parking lot, babbling incoherently, back to the relative safety of the bar. I suspected that Matthew had been a decent man in life, since he was a nice companion, solicitous and pleasant in his current condition. Which always made me wonder…

"Matthew—"

"Ah, jeez, Caroline, not again."

I could see the sorrow and the shame flicker through his brown eyes as he looked away, hiding his feelings as always. "Matthew, you are a good man, and you should be somewhere else, somewhere where you can make a difference, do something with your—"

"My life?" Matthew grinned. "I guess I already blew that."

"With your kind and decent spir—character."

"Ain't no angel, Caroline." The younger man flashed an embarrassed smile and stubbed his boot toe against the new carpeting the library had put in last year. He also stepped back, out of the way of a mother and two small boys who had come for the chocolate chip cookies and punch. The youngest boy, about 5, looked up at Matthew, who just smiled and saluted him. The child continued to stare after Matthew as his mother led them back to their seats for the second half of the presentation. Matthew waved at him, and the child somewhat tentatively made a little wave back, his eyes big.

Matthew sighed long and hard. "Amazing what they still remember at that age, still can see. I heard tell children can hear the heavenly choir until they get so many adults telling 'em it's their imagination."

"Did your parents tell you that, Matthew?"

"Naw, saw it on a TV show. Kinda made sense to me."

"Me, too." I sighed as long and hard as he had. "I just don't understand why we have to end up at the library. I surely expected something different than this existence."

"Well, yeah, me too—but personally, I think this is fine,

considering where I most likely would have ended up." He hung his head sheepishly and studied the carpeting before adding softly, "If you know what I mean."

"Oh, Matthew, you really must stop denigrating yourself—"

He suddenly pushed forward, waving goodbye. "Hey, I think I saw Stella headed for the stacks—gotta run, Carolie! Don't think too hard, you might hurt yourself someday!"

I turned to Margie, who gave me "the look." "Don't start on me," she said. "I don't know why we're here, and I don't know how to get anyplace else. Maybe we just weren't good enough."

"Well, for heaven's sake, after all you did for the church and the community during your life, I'd think there are a good number that have less to offer on their account than you do."

Margie blinked, her mouth setting in a thin line as she tightened her grip on her emotions. "Don't, Caroline. Just don't." She drew a deep breath—more out of habit, I suppose—and forced herself to calm. "It's best not to think about it too hard. I'm just glad to be here. There are worse places." And with that, she turned and shuffled off toward the lobby, where I knew she liked to try rearranging the displays at night, to the dismay of the early librarian every morning. Well, everyone had to have a hobby, especially in this place. There wasn't much else to do.

The fact was, there wasn't much to do in a town where they rolled up the sidewalks by 11 p.m. Even the hospital was a bit of a bore—unless there was a big accident up on Highway 50. Then, you might find yourself comforting someone in the emergency room who was wavering between this world and the next. That was eminently satisfying and made me feel as if there really were some reason I was still here. But in the end, this wandering around looking for something to do while waiting for a call from either the Pearly Gates, or the other place, or just lovely, peaceful darkness, became about as frustrating as life had been. As the ghost hunters began the second half of their presentation, I decided I had had enough of this nonsense. I needed some answers.

So, the next morning, I drifted down Main Street and took a hard left on Market until I found myself on the grass beside the old stone structure of the First Presbyterian Church. The interior hadn't changed since I'd moved into town forty years ago, and truthfully hadn't changed much since the 1930s. I said hello to a few church members who had "passed" long before I did and who apparently liked to hang out in the narthex and fellowship hall, pretending to drink coffee again. I was tempted to ask them for insights, but like Margie, most really didn't want to talk about it. So I took the stairs up to the new offices. Thank goodness they had torn down the crumbling old office building and put the staff over here on the top floor, just below the bats in the belfry so to speak.

I'd been a member for many years, long enough to meet the new young associate pastor. He was sitting at his desk in the office at the top of the stairs, typing away furiously at his laptop. Must be the one week of the month when he was allowed to demonstrate his amazing powers of sermon-making. Also the one Sunday of the month when attendance tended to take a nosedive.

He was still working on his pastoral skills. Some people liked his new approach, but others—of all ages—found his new ideas and interactive sermons just a bit too "personal." I had enjoyed them although I still leaned toward tradition. Curious, I hovered over his shoulder a moment, reading his efforts until he paused, looked around a bit mystified, then shuddered as if someone had walked over his grave. Politely I stepped back. No point in scaring him, and I really didn't think I was going to get a useful answer out of a youngster.

So, I drifted down the hall, looking for Michael, the older pastor who had been there for a goodly number of years, and had, I think, officiated at my funeral. I couldn't remember exactly because it all happened so fast after I passed, and given that I didn't have a lot of family in the area, I lost interest after checking in to see who was there. I really was more interested in exploring my new existence and trying to figure out where the hell the "stairway to heaven" was supposed to be.

Slipping into Michael's large, comfortable office with old, worn chairs, the big bookcases and large window where sun was streaming in, I plopped down in the chair opposite his desk which sat to one side, facing the door. The soft exhale of air from the old pseudo-leather seat cushion disturbed a single sheet of paper that had been dangling precariously from one of the many stacks of papers, books, notices, etc. on his desk. It took flight, drifting slowly, erratically down to the floor beside my chair.

Michael was lounging back in his old wood office chair, reading something intently, worn reading glasses perched on his nose, one finger stroking his pepper-and-salt short beard. At the movement of the paper, he looked up, scanning the room like a dog on the scent. Suddenly, he sat forward, office chair groaning with years of abuse from his large but not fat frame, and laid his book on the desk, facedown. He peered toward the door expectantly.

I frowned at such treatment of a book, but said nothing. I wasn't sure it would have made a difference. Instead, I waited to see if he was—well, I could tell he was aware something was up. I began to have second thoughts. Michael wasn't a spring chicken anymore; I didn't want to give the poor man a heart attack or a stroke. I was about to get up and leave when, after a second or two, his gaze focused on my chair, looking straight at me. He frowned a moment, squinting, then smiled broadly.

"Caroline! I was wondering when you'd turn up," he said softly, still smiling.

Well, I will tell you, I was shocked. It was the first time anyone had used my name in a way that made sound echo on the air. I felt suddenly as if I were … well, almost naked, although I could see that I was wearing my favorite green dress. I wondered if I had the matching necklace and earrings on as well, and reached up self-consciously to feel for them, without finding my ear. I didn't know how I would look to anyone. We just didn't worry about such things down at the library or in the hospital, etc. I guess we saw ourselves and each other as we expected ourselves to be, without really being aware of what that was—or caring. But this … I could feel the air on my skin, the sensation of my clothes hanging on my body, the pressure of my hair pulled up in a loose bun. All of a sudden, I felt very *present*—simply because someone alive acknowledged my existence.

I studied my hands lying in my lap. I didn't see any blood, which was good, because I was suddenly reminded it had been a car accident … I mean, I really didn't want to upset anyone. Oddly enough my hands looked, well, odd. One moment older and puffy, knobbed joints, age spots—and the next second, smooth, young and slim, and then …

"Caroline, it's good to see you." Michael grinned as I jerked my head up to meet his gaze. See? I wondered exactly what he did see. I felt almost as if someone were looking through my bones as he peered at me intently.

"Are you…" I stopped. My voice sounded like a distant echo, a bell on the water. It had been … well, only a month or two, hadn't it? All at once, it seemed a long time since I had heard my own voice, or anyone else had. Could he hear it?

He nodded as if to encourage me to go on. "Can you hear me?" I said.

"Oh yes," he nodded.

I was flabbergasted, I'll tell you. "Like … like before?"

"Well, it's a little different. More like a bit of an echo in my head." He leaned back in his chair. "So, how's it going?"

I was a little taken aback by his attitude, or rather the lack of it. I mean, I was dead, right? Didn't that deserve just a little more surprise or dismay? This mundane reaction seemed a bit disrespectful. I mean, I didn't want or need him to be grief-stricken or terrified or anything, But a little acknowledgement of the bizarreness of the circumstance would have been nice, or at least appropriate. I mean, really.

"Are you," I hesitated. "Are you all right ? I mean, I didn't quite expect you to be so calm about it."

He just smiled in amusement. "Let's just say this isn't my first rodeo." He settled back in his chair as if enjoying an afternoon tea at the Botanical Gardens. "I saw Bob the other day. He said to say hello."

"Bob Hartman?" I babbled. He had passed over several years ago. "Are you telling me you talk to the dead all the time?"

"Not *all* the time. I talk to the living quite a bit too, as you well know. I've missed our debates since you, ah … left."

"Well, we can continue one right here and right now," I huffed. "This isn't what I expected."

"What did you expect?"

"Well," I threw up my hands, "Well, not this!"

"Then what *did* you expect?" Michael's gaze fixed on mine quite pointedly. "As I recall, you had a number of theories about what happens next, and were a bit unsure which one you gravitated to." He rubbed his forefinger over the edge of his beard around his lips. "You had a lot of questions about all the options, and didn't much care for any of my feeble answers. In fact, you couldn't seem to decide which ones you preferred."

"Well, it's not really relevant what I preferred, is it?" I fluffed up in indignation at the very thought. "After all, isn't this all His plan?" I gestured to the ceiling. "I thought we were supposed to await judgement. And then . . ." I waved my hand around uncertainly. "And then, and then . . ."

"You get your ticket punched for a particular destination?"

Michael's blue eyes were dancing with a bit of mirth, and it set my blood boiling. Well, it set something boiling. We had always talked frankly with each other, and shared a good laugh over some theological matters that might have scandalized someone more conservative. But really, this was going too far.

"Now, see here. I will not be treated like this. I came here with a serious question. A very serious question. After all, I am dead. And it's high time for somebody, somewhere to make a decision about the situation." I slammed my fist down on his desk. There wasn't any pain, nor, I thought, any noise—but Michael jumped. His eyes were on me, and for one moment I saw a flicker of dismay. Then he patted the air in front of him gently, as if calming a child.

"All right, I'll do what I can but please stay calm. Don't get . . . overheated." He glanced out his door, into the hallway. In the silence, I could hear the faint clack of the laptop's keys in the front office. Michael sat back, assured his younger colleague was blissfully unaware. "Andrew isn't really ready for things like that."

"Like what?" I demanded. A pastor should be ready for a discussion of the hereafter, but Michael hesitated. "What?" I demanded.

Michael patted the air in front of him calmingly with both hands now. "It's just that you're, um, well, glowing. Kind of a nimbus of light all around you when you get excited. Just sort of a … lingering effect."

"Lingering effect?"

Michael looked uncomfortable, which was unusual for him. But then, I suppose talking to the dead was rather uncomfortable, even for a minister. But he was squinting, looking aside as if he couldn't quite bear to look at me. He waved a hand in apology, and tried to explain. "It's just rather bright…"

"Bright," I repeated, still confused.

He blinked and held up a hand, shielding his eyes slightly. "Probably from the, ah, … cremation."

I stared at him, horrified suddenly. My sense of self began to disintegrate at the reality of my situation. I really wasn't here, was I, although I had felt like I was until now. Was I? I looked down at my hands, expecting to see flames. Instead, I saw cold, white hands, beginning to fade away to translucent fingers, and then, bones. I stared at the skeletal digits as the flesh faded and moved up my arm, revealing wrist bones, then the long curve of the ulna, like something rising up out of a misty pool of water …

"Now, don't try that with me," Michael said firmly, wagging a warning finger at me. "I've seen it before and it's not helpful." I could tell he was scared as I put my bony hand to my face and felt nothing but bone under my fingertips. I wanted to cry, but I didn't seem to have any tears.

"Now, calm down!" Michael patted the air again between us with a nervous glance out the office door into the hallway. "I want to be here for you, Caroline, but for heaven's sakes, get control before somebody else comes up these stairs and keels over from a heart attack. I don't need any other funerals this month. Four is more than enough."

"Any others? There weren't any for months before me and it's only been a few weeks since..."

"Oh, Caroline," Michael sighed gently, and gave me an endearing smile of affection. "It's been a bit longer than you might realize."

I hesitated. "How long?"

He pursed his lips and looked off, calculating. "Well, let's see... ah, fifteen months?" He looked back at me hopefully.

"Oh," I said weakly. "I'm so sorry. It seems like..."

"Yesterday? Yes, that's what most people tell me."

"So, you... have a lot of people here, asking questions, like me?"

"Well, some do and some don't. Some just apparently go on. They don't call, they don't write—" He grinned a moment at the joke, then grew somber at my look and shrugged. "Others stick around for a while. They seem to enjoy it, but eventually..." He waggled his head, as if it were a choice between the white or the red wine at a party.

"But why me?" I suddenly felt like a failure. Others were going about their business—going on to wherever they were supposed to be—and I was just wandering around like a fool? Like a... an... unbeliever? I felt cold. Perhaps this was the way I would remain, for eternity. "Why am I still here, Michael?"

"Well," Michael composed his face to a somber consideration of the question. "Perhaps you didn't feel like leaving right away. Maybe you had something to do? A relationship that needed tending? A worry about someone or something left behind, like the cats?" He added reassuringly, "They're all fine, you know."

I nodded without really thinking about it. I was distracted, running through the last weeks and months of my life, wondering if there was something I had done, or said, or left undone, or … some terrible thing I'd done without thinking that had barred me from any future beyond this life. But nothing came to mind. On the other hand, did I still have a mind?

"Caroline."

I looked up into those kind blue eyes. I felt like a sailor in a vast ocean, clinging to a life preserver in that calm, familiar gaze. I was so grateful that he knew me, knew my name, remembered me at least … and wasn't afraid. But then the anxiety began to creep over me at such thoughts. I mean, was I even here? Or was I just a memory of myself? A residual haunting as the paranormal group called it, like a recording of the past? Was my soul gone? Was there anything left except some kind of lingering delusion that I still existed?

"I don't know what to do," I whispered helplessly. Michael's soft voice cut through my despair.

"Caroline, do you remember our discussions?"

I nodded like a child, and gazed up at him, facing the teacher, awaiting my doom. Michael rested his elbows on the desk, steepled his fingers together, and gave me a gentle smile.

"Remember when I told you that some people think that you get what you expect in the afterlife?" He asked softly.

"Well, I didn't expect this!"

"No, but what did you expect? I remember you reading and wanting to talk about all kinds of possibilities—reincarnation, 'sleeping at the foot of the throne,' lying comatose in a grave, returning as a raindrop, simply going out like a candle, Elysian fields, Hades, etc." He chuckled gently. "You were probably the most literate explorer of the afterlife I've met in my churches. But did any particular view appeal to you more than others—something you wanted more, something that felt like paradise?"

I wracked my memories for an answer, but realized suddenly that all I recalled of "heaven" in my musings was the vague, fluffy sense of something golden, peaceful and filled with all the things I'd lost over the years—and a sense of being perfectly, eternally, safe and loved. But in a kind of marshmallow way. I gestured helplessly, still trying to find concrete memory that didn't involve silly white robes and harps. After a few minutes of silence, Michael's voice nudged me again.

"Well, you know you don't have to make a decision immediately. You can continue to hang at the library. A lot of people do. Or you could join some of the old gang here once in a while..." When I didn't answer, he suggested brightly, as one might placate a child, "You could take a world tour, explore your options."

I was appalled, and a little frightened. "Alone?"

Michael's mouth worked a moment, as he struggled to state the obvious as gently as possible. "Well, Caroline, I don't think anything is going to happen to you that could be ... any worse ... than what's already happened. Hm?"

He paused a moment, and frowned. "But I'd stay out of some of the darker spots on the planet. They have some different views on the afterlife. Just stick to the well-traveled routes, places you've wanted to go. Don't get led astray by any … thing." He brightened. "Maybe you could get a group from the library to go along!"

"You know about the others?"

Michael shrugged deprecatingly. "Well, I'm in there frequently. It's kind of hard to miss."

I grasped at that. "Why? Why can you see me and nobody else can? Or at least nobody I've encountered yet will admit it."

"My grandmothers were Scottish and Russian, and both had what most people would call 'second sight.' And a few other reasons like that. They talked to the departed when I was a very little child, and I rather thought it was all very natural."

"A world tour," I murmured.

"You always wanted to travel, but with the cats, it wasn't really possible." Michael sat back in his chair. "Now you're free, free to explore some of the great cathedrals, temples, other spots of faith and belief. Hang out with some of the old masters who might be still around. Try out the British Museum and Library. A lot of rare books, might find some answers that satisfy you."

"Satisfy me?" I tensed in my chair. "What does my satisfaction have to do with it? I thought there was some kind of … judgement."

"Well, as we said, perhaps it's a matter of choice. It's possible everyone—everywhere—is waiting for you to decide where you want to go and what you want to do with eternity. Surely how we decide to spend eternity is at least as important as the things we do with one lifetime." Michael's eyes shifted to the corners of the room in memory as he smiled wryly. "I had a young lady many years ago at another church who told me she was thinking of coming back as a chicken."

"A chicken!?"

He grinned. "Yes. She said that it was appealing to her because first, she wouldn't have to spend her whole life worrying about paying bills, and that chickens seemed to have a simple life, and that even when they died, they fed other creatures which she thought would be a good use of her mortal remains, and it all seemed very quiet and simple after a rather difficult life."

"Did she—?" The question popped out before I could stop it.

"Well," Michael shrugged. "I don't really know, since I'm still here and she isn't, but I have to say, I always say a little prayer of thanks over every piece of meat at the potlucks." His eyes grew soft. "Truthfully, I'm eating a lot more vegetarian stuff since then. But she seemed quite content with the prospect."

"A chicken." I struggled to consider it, and actually found myself relaxing into the idea.

"Well, it's just her personal thought. I don't know what she decided in the end."

"Well," I tried to form the question that was awkwardly nagging at me. "What about hell? Hades, the fiery lake? Doesn't anybody go there?"

"Oh, I suspect a lot of people do—if they can't see past it. Tell you the truth, I had a man once in my early ministry who almost took me with him, when he was dying in the hospital— he was terrified of dying, of punishment—"

Michael paused. I waited, wide eyed, and thinking of Matthew, finally understanding why he hung out at the library with us old biddies. He was afraid.

Michael looked up from his memory, saw me watching, and smiled. "Oh, he survived, and I was called to a new church about then, so I don't really know what happened. But I think it's really more like Swedenborg says, it's less of a judgement or punishment than a choice. Some people stay where they feel comfortable, even though it's not a good place. It's simply the one they know." He chuckled. "Gives new meaning to the 'devil you know is preferable to the one you don't.'"

Sobering again, he seemed sad. "They just can't get past their own issues or accept grace or think they're worthy, despite Christ's promises." I thought of Matthew as Michael continued, "I hope that relatively few actually choose that route. But some people are very ... determined, as you know. Downright rigid."

I gave him a sour look. "I am not now, nor have I ever been, rigid."

"Oh no, not you. Forceful, yes. But rigid, no, no." He smiled mischievously. "I was thinking of some other people."

"Mildred Hampmeister," I suggested tartly. "Also known as one of the kitchen Nazis by the teenagers."

He tried not to smile. I had to restrain a smile myself and said, "Best not to speak ill of the dead, I suppose, eh?"

Michael snorted in amusement and nodded. "Mildred was never in the least bit of doubt where she was going, even if she had to batter down the gates. A formidable woman. I often pray for St. Peter and the angels."

We both broke out laughing.

A face appeared at the office door, which had been standing ajar during all this. Andrew peered around the corner, scanning the room for a visitor, his printed sermon in his hands. He seemed a bit disconcerted not to see anyone. Or at least me, sitting about three feet in front of him. I wondered if he would try to sit in my lap since I had the only chair facing Michael's desk. And truthfully, I couldn't help but wonder what would happen if I somehow materialized ...

I saw Michael give me the look. I smiled sweetly back. He nervously tried to focus on Andrew and on me at the same time. That made him look a bit … odd. Andrew studied his mentor with a worried frown and started into the room.

"I thought I heard you talking to someone."

Michael shrugged and tapped his book still lying facedown on the desk. "Just reading out loud."

As Andrew made a move for the chair I was sitting in, Michael rose from his seat abruptly. "I'm about to go find some lunch, Andrew. Why don't you join us—er, me?"

"Are you meeting someone?" Andrew asked hopefully. He was very new in town, and I knew he must be lonely.

"Well," said Michael with a glance at me. "You never know who you'll meet."

"I wanted to ask you a few things about my sermon," Andrew said cautiously. "I'm trying to make it a bit more … well, like yours." He blushed. "I know people aren't very happy with my past efforts."

"Not at all. People just need to get over their expectations and allow themselves to explore new ideas." Michael looked directly at me as he ushered Andrew back toward the door and hall. "Why don't you print out what you've got so far, and make two copies. We'll look them over while eating. Let me get my hat and my phone. And afterward," he called as Andrew hurried back to his own office, "we'll stop by the library. I need to pick out a couple of books for an old friend."

I rose. Michael popped his old-style alpine hat on his head—an affectation in a day and age when hats were *déclassé*. He paused as he shoved his phone into his pocket

"I'm sorry, Caroline. I couldn't think of any other way to get him out of here—although I dare say you could have!"

I grinned. I was feeling immensely better, hopeful even.

"Give it some thought. Decide what and where you want to be. But there's no rush." He grinned back at me. "Eternity can wait."

I hesitated. "I'd like to see some of the pets again, and of course, my parents and all … but by now, who knows if…" I hesitated to voice my fears.

"It's not like there's an expiration date, or that they're going anywhere. Unless of course, they decide to come back for another round."

"Do you think it's all that … simple?" I whispered. "You get what you expect?"

He shrugged. "I'm not the one to ask, dear. You know, just because you're dead doesn't mean you can't talk to Him anymore."

I started to cry. I hadn't spoken to God since I'd died. I hadn't been sure I had a right to, since things didn't work out quite as I had assumed.

Michael patted my shoulder, or tried to, and sighed. "The ones I worry about are the ones who think they have to wait in their graves, waiting until they're 'called.' Kind of like people waiting to see if they're 'called' to the ministry. Not sure if they're 'good enough' and all that." He leaned forward conspiratorially, "If we all had to wait to do anything until we were 'good enough,' I suspect the living and dead would never get anywhere, in this life or the next. Not what Jesus was about. As Paul says, 'He died for us while we were yet sinners.'"

"'And he descended into hell,'" I quoted the Apostles' Creed, suddenly realizing things I'd never realized before. "Descended into hell…" I murmured, starting for the door. I heard Andrew yelling something to Michael from the copier room.

"Take that world tour and give it some thought." Michael grinned as we both headed for the stairs. "And send me a postcard or two, just for fun. I would love to see how that goes over when whoever is in the office that week as secretary shares it on the church grapevine."

I held back as Andrew and he clattered down the steps, then I headed back to the library walking on air. Literally. I had always stayed on terra firma, even though I couldn't really feel it under my feet. Now, I floated, feeling free, having the whole of eternity as it were, laid out at my feet like a gift.

Author Comments:

I rarely read ghost stories, since I have a sensitivity to the paranormal and don't like opening the door to negative experiences. When I do read them, I prefer the Victorian gothics of Louisa May Alcott, and the spookier stories of Mary Roberts Rhinehart. So, not knowing where to begin in writing a ghost story, I just typed, "I am ghost." So far, so good, I thought, without any idea where to go next. I just let my thoughts wander on their natural course, and ended up somewhat naturally exploring an idea I have long held—which is that we may get what we expect when we die. As a Christian, I have no doubts about a forgiving God (who is willing to receive anyone who comes seeking) but I have no clear idea about what lies ahead, although I have had many messages from loved ones who have passed on—enough to know death isn't the end. I found my characters naturally sorting out the possibilities. I ended up very pleased with the way this story ended up, and hope it offers those who think only in terms of "up or down" a new perspective.

Moving On
by John Hanford

Vietnam, III Corps, 1967

Bravo Company, a mechanized infantry unit, was hauling ass to reach a grunt unit that was hit heavily the previous night. It was mid-February. Twenty year-old Steve Tresmer, T to his buddies, was driving a track, i.e. an armored personnel carrier, that was third in the column of tracked vehicles. As a corporal he was the ranking man on his vehicle. The soldiers rode on the top of rather than inside the APC to give them a better chance of survival in case of a land mine. Their track had its name painted in white letters on each side: To Sir Charles with Love. Most of the others also had names given by their soldiers. The painting of names on vehicles was frowned upon by commanding officers.

Steve partook in an activity he often did on long drives: he designed in his head the car he would purchase upon his return to the world. In his letters home, he would ask his mother to send him the advertisements from the local Plymouth dealers. He wanted to buy something with a 426 cubic inch Hemi engine, a monstrously impractical car, albeit perfect for street drag racing. He sensed he might have to settle for a 383. More than the car dealer ads his mother sent, Steve most liked reading his mother's words and seeing her handwriting. Her script was another unique thing about her that he relished, a connection of sorts to her from his childhood.

As they rounded a bend, the company saw a small village about a klick ahead. Due to their haste, the CO apparently had determined to barrel through the village on the one dirt road with no prior recon. At about five hundred meters, Bravo Company began taking automatic weapons and small arms fire. The column immediately returned fire with their mounted .50 cals and individual weapons while simultaneously diverting APCs to each side of the road. The vehicles spread out, putting ten to fifteen meters space between them. The mortar track retreated a couple of hundred meters behind the line and rapidly prepared a fire mission. Within two minutes of first coming under fire, 81 mm high-explosive rounds were raining down near and then into the village. After another two minutes, the CO ordered a ceasefire.

Tresmer could not hear any more gunfire or the whizzing of rounds flying by. After another couple of minutes, Stanley Jackson, Jacks, the squad leader, announced over the radio that all the hooches in the village were to be cleared. Shit, thought Steve, why the fuck can't we just drive around this piss-ant shithole and be on our way. Jackson then ordered To Sir Charles with Love to proceed slowly on pace with the other tracks. No additional rounds were directed at the American unit. The bad guys had likely fled.

Soldiers began dismounting their vehicles when they reached the perimeter of the village in order to search the buildings. Drivers and .50 gunners stayed on board. However, Tresmer knew Mike Kluska had sprained his ankle just that morning. He motioned the gunner to take his place at the controls and for Kluska to man the machine gun. He then jumped off the vehicle, making sure he had at least two bandoliers of ammo wrapped around his chest.

He ran toward Jacks. The *chieu hois*, surrendered Viet Cong fighters who were now working as scouts for the Americans, were yelling for everyone to exit the buildings. Slowly, villagers did just that as scouts roughly rounded them up. They then gave the CO the all clear, and he directed his soldiers to begin clearing the dozen or so small buildings. Jacks ordered Tresmer and a couple of his soldiers to clear a longish structure clad in flattened Number 10 cans. It appeared to be the only multi-room place in the village. This building was on the edge of the hamlet. Upon entering the structure, Steve saw three doors presumably opening to three rooms. He had one soldier cover two of the doors. To clear the other room, one GI pulled the door open, T rolled in a grenade, slammed the door shut, and hit the deck, pulling down the other soldier with him. The explosion blasted grenade fragments through the thin wall, and then toppled the wall onto them. He quickly pushed off debris and saw there was no one inside the room. He checked the guy next to him and saw him dazed but okay.

Tresmer knew then that grenades weren't the best option for the two remaining rooms. He got to his feet, pulled up the other soldier, and quickly ran to where the third soldier was guarding the two doors. He pointed to his M-16 shaking his head "yes" then to his grenades while shaking his head "no" to indicate not to use them. He motioned for the first soldier, a newbie he didn't know, to open the door. As soon as the door opened a crack, he sprayed the room with a sustained burst, reloaded, and motioned for the soldier to open the door further. He again sprayed the room as he and a second soldier stepped in. The room was also empty.

The same drill would be used to clear the final room. Tresmer reloaded a second time as he stepped to the door. The newbie slipped the door open a crack, T fired a burst, reloaded, and the door was opened fully as he sent in another burst. They entered the room. Lying on the floor was a pregnant woman clutching to her bosom a young child who had the back of his head blown off. She offered a terrified, pained look to the soldiers. "Shit," exclaimed Tresmer; the other soldier had frozen and just stared. Blood spurted from the woman's neck as she violently jerked. Instinctively, T fired twice more into the dying woman. From underneath a table, another small child ran to her. Nerves tripped again as he shot him twice before the boy reached her. He saw the kid's bloody cranial tissue splash against the floor. Now Steve also just stood there and simply stared.

Suddenly, he felt someone grab the back of his fatigue collar. "Tresmer, it happens." It was Jacks. T was unsure how long he had stood there. "Get back to your track. We're outta here. Go on now. We're done here." Steve turned, glared at Jacks, then made it back to his track.

He didn't remember getting back to his vehicle. The next thing he did remember was driving and smelling something vomit-like. He glanced down at his fatigues. A large stain covered his front. That's when he puked again. He stopped the vehicle and stood to see if he had been wounded. No wounds. Just puke.

Twelve days after this incident, the following entry was made into the Daily Log of the 1st Battalion (M), 5th Infantry, 25th Infantry Division:

02/28/70-#4: 1216 hours, the lead APC of a resupply convoy headed to Dau Tieng base from B Co. lager detonated an explosive device on a dirt road running through the Michelin Plantation at XT 557512. The APC was completely destroyed and it was believed seven (7) Bobcats KIA. At 1250 hours, a dust-off was requested for two (2) Bobcats who were wounded and in shock. Graves registration personnel were called to the location for recovery of body parts. GR could not definitively determine number of KIA. This information pending. The explosive device was estimated to be in the 500 pound category (unexploded US ordinance???). The two (2) individuals were dusted off to 45th SH (Tay Ninh). One M-548 TVR also damaged when ramp from APC was blown backwards into the 548, knocking out its final drive.

Independence, Missouri, 2020

"Hey, you geniuses go play in traffic…with blindfolds," Deryl said quietly not glancing up from his coffee. It was his response to some ribbing he received from the other guys. No real offense was taken by anyone for the ribbing nor the rebuke. The group moved on.

This was Boys Club, a Vietnam veterans' support group that met twice monthly at the DAV on 40 Highway. The service organization let the guys use its conference room. The local VA where the PTSD clinic was located claimed not to have room for these meetings even though a conference room in that building sat entirely idle for four out of five weekdays. These Vietnam vets were used to being shunted to the side by the VA, used to being seen as disposable by the government. Fortunately, through one of the member's connections with the Disabled American Veteran's organization, the group held its meetings there.

The group usually shot the shit for a few minutes then often discussed VA policy issues that affected the health care they received from that agency. All these vets depended upon it for such care. After a few minutes of gabbing, the boys, all men in their seventies, got down to their most important business—checking in with each member to see how things were going. Anniversaries of bad times in-country were particularly troublesome for some of the men. Advice, brainstorming, empathy, and ribbing were doled out as deemed appropriate. The group in total had twenty-nine members but had stabilized with eight to twelve in attendance regularly at each session. One member had passed away in the past couple of years, and no new vets had joined.

The VA PTSD therapists knew of the group and personally approved of its intent. They would occasionally suggest to new patients that they inquire about joining. Boys Club was self regulated and the members approved or disapproved candidates for membership. Although veterans from conflicts after the Vietnam War were occasionally admitted, they never stayed more than a few sessions. Candidates would 'audition,' which consisted of answering various questions asked by some of the guys to prove the candidate was actually a combat vet and also that he wasn't a complete asshole. A spokesman, usually Doc, customarily let the candidate know by telephone whether he'd be welcome to return.

Many of the members socialized little beyond Boys Club and had grown increasingly reclusive through the years. Most had moderate to severe PTSD with the trust issues, especially of strangers, that went hand-in-hand with that condition. Among the vets, there was a definite comfort level and camaraderie, needs they could not readily have met elsewhere. Bosley, a happy spirit and Joe's mongrel service dog, was just another one of the guys.

At the first meeting in December, the guys were in the shooting-the-shit stage of the get-together. This part was often more animated than later stages of meetings; today it was particularly so, perhaps due to the fact that three of the men brought donuts. Occasionally, one brought a dozen, which were quickly and appropriately disposed of. On this day, as each new box arrived unexpectedly, the banter grew louder and the guys a bit more lively.

There was a knock on the door. No one heard it over the racket. Then there was another knock.

"Is that someone knocking?" asked Doc.

"Yup. I'll check," said Herb, who was closest to the door. The men barely stopped eating and yakking.

After a couple of minutes, Herb closed the door and informed the group, "There's a guy out here saying Dr. Kent told him our group might be good for him. I told him it's a closed group, but what do you guys think?" In a lowered voice so as not to be overheard by the individual waiting outside in the hallway, Herb followed with, "He looks pretty ate up."

"A closed group is a closed group," said Don. "What's to not understand? Besides, Dr. Kent's been gone from the VA for six months now."

"Don't be a dick," said Rabbit. "This boy might really need a little something. At one point or the other all of us were the FNG just needing a little something. We were all outside the door our first time here. Let's hear his story."

Upon hearing Rabbit, Herb said, "I'm inviting him in,

gentlemen. Let's hear him out." Herb opened the door and saw the new guy on his way out of the building. Through the conference room's floor-to-ceiling windows the guys could see Herb head down the hallway in the direction of the building exit and heard him say, "Hey, brother, don't leave. Come on in. Yeah, it's okay. C'mon."

After a few seconds, Herb held open the door. The very pale gentleman who came through it was balding but had gray locks down to his shoulders. He was tall, stooped, seriously underweight, and had a very noticeable head tremor. He held a ball cap in his hands.

"Hey, fellas, I'm Steve Tresmer. I appreciate you inviting me in."

Doc, a former Marine medic and the notetaker for the group, stood. "Hi, Steve, I'm Dave Eckhart. To introduce ourselves to you, we'll tell you our name, service, and dates in-country. I'm a Marine and was in I Corps as a medic from late sixty-seven to early sixty-nine. Oh, and please have a seat; we're beyond casual here." The tired looking newcomer sat in a chair with his back to the wall. One by one the others provided their information. Then the grilling began.

"This here's a closed group and we're not accepting new members," blurted Don.

"Hey, guys, I didn't know that. Dr. Kent told me about you men and suggested I come here to see if this would work out for me. I'm sorry. I had no idea. I'll just go on and leave."

With a smile, Don pressed, "Buddy, Dr. Kent left the VA six months ago."

"Well ... I ... I'm sorry, I forgot your name ... well, it took me ten months to ahh ... to just get the courage to come here."

Doc shot Don a stern look and interjected, "Hell, Steve, that's probably the case for a number of us. Dr. Kent had to coax me for a couple of months to join. Jim I believe took at least twice that long before he came in." Doc offered a welcoming smile. "No big deal. So, Steve, tell us who you were with in Vietnam and what you did."

After a few seconds, with a flat affect and monotone voice, Steve slowly revealed the general details: He was a rifleman assigned to a mechanized infantry unit of the 25th Division. Then he became more specific. He spent nearly eight months with Bravo Company before being medevaced from a rubber plantation near Dau Tieng. While telling his story he mostly kept his eyes downward except for a few glances at Don. He paused for at least a minute as if searching for words. "That chopper probably had more KIA than wounded. The crew chief probably didn't…"

Doc interjected, breaking Steve's mounting tension. "Hey, brother, you don't have to tell us anything else. Everyone in here has an anniversary or two. Thanks, Steve."

With those words, Steve slumped back into his chair, continued looking at the floor, and slowly let forth a huge exhalation through pursed lips. He managed a wan smile and nodded his head "yes" a couple of times at the floor. Doc explained the format of the meetings. The session eventually got to the individual check-ins with each member. When it became Steve's turn, he excused himself to go to the restroom. Once he was clear of earshot, various members began giving their opinions about the suitability of admitting Steve to the group.

"That boy is spooked fer sure," said Rabbit. "I know telling new people about that place is tough on everybody, but it was like this was his first time saying that shit."

Herb spoke next. "Maybe we were that shook up our first time here. For me, I wasn't about to go telling y'all about bat-shit crazy stuff right off. I'm kind of surprised he went there. But I agree with Rabbit, Steve's hurtin'."

A few of the others offered their take on Steve and his story. After ten minutes, Doc spoke up. "I'm going to go check on him. He's been in the crapper a long time."

"I'll bet he left," said Don, "and I won't be surprised either."

"Well aren't you Mr. Compassion," replied Joe.

"Hey man, I'm just sayin'. Christ, I'm not sayin' it's a mortal sin. I just don't think this dude is up for our group."

Doc stood, shot another look at Don and left to check on Steve. He returned moments later. "Guys, ol' Steve-o has done left the building."

Predictably, Don blurted out, "I told you. And, he won't be back either."

"Well, if he does come back, I say we let him in. Looks like he needs some guys to lean on a little," said Herb.

"I agree," added Doc.

All except Don were also in favor of Herb's proposal. Having finished the day's business, the men filed out, chatting in twos and threes as they slowly walked to their vehicles.

As was his habit, Doc arrived a few minutes before the scheduled start of the next meeting. He enjoyed talking one-on-one with whomever might be there. To his surprise, seated at the first chair closest to the door was Steve Tresmer, who started a bit as Doc opened the door.

"Hey, Steve. I'm glad you made it."

"Thanks, Doc. I wasn't sure if I should come back, still not sure I can fit in with you guys."

"Hey, brother, that's our specialty in this group: not fitting in. That's the beauty of the group, we're all misfits. You're fine."

"Don seemed a bit put off…"

"That's what I mean about being misfits. Don is just a little more mis-fitted than the rest of us." Doc gave a reassuring laugh. "He'll warm up. He can be a horse's ass sometimes, but that's his personality. He needs this group, just like the rest of us, so he gets a little protective of it. No big deal. Just like all the different guys in a typical unit: not all are the friendliest, but when the shit starts flyin' you can count on 'em."

"Okay." Steve sat back and kept his head down.

Doc was unsure if he had gotten through to him. Gradually, nine more members came in and caught up with each other. Handshakes were usually part of the greeting, and all came by to shake Steve's hand. The one's who hadn't been there the previous meeting introduced themselves. Doc noticed Steve didn't smile but at least had his head up and conversed quietly with Ron. Ron was doing all the talking. Steve nodded occasionally.

The meeting progressed to the check-in roundabout. Steve listened to each man, but didn't offer anything to anyone. He spent the time tearing and re-tearing a napkin until the pieces were minuscule, and for over forty minutes rapidly bobbed his left knee up and down. There was just one member to go before it would be Steve's turn. Without a word, he left the meeting. The guys could see he went into the restroom.

"I don't know about this dude. He may need more than we can give him. He's one of the more spooked guys I've seen in years," Don said. "I didn't think he'd be back, but he came. I'll give him that. He's likely beyond this group. I'm not sure we need his kind in here."

"'His kind.' What kinda shit is that? Let's just see what he has to say," replied Herb. "We really don't know anything about him except he came here looking for support."

"Yeah," said Doc. "Maybe…" Steve reentered the room, cutting Doc off midsentence.

Doc inquired, "So, Steve how's things been going this week?"

"It's been going the same this week as it's been going for as long as I can remember. I've never married. I'm homeless. I talk to no one, like ever. I've never talked about the terrible things I did in-country. That story about getting dusted off, that was not even bad for me; that was a relief. At least I knew I couldn't hurt anyone again. It's getting near the end for me, gents. I have to get stuff out to maybe find peace, even though that's the last thing I deserve after the shit I've done." These were by far the most words Steve had spoken to the group. He paused, blew his nose, and continued. "Saying these things won't make me less of a monster or coward, but I'll know that someone else heard my story. I don't know what difference it'll make, but it's something that I sense needs doing." Steve's head tremor had noticeably intensified while speaking, but as he spoke, he looked around the room and made eye contact with everyone present.

"You mean in forty-five, fifty years, you've never talked to anyone about the things that happened to you in the shit?" asked Don.

"Yeah, that's right. I've been bouncing around here and there, not staying anywhere or around anyone too long. Biggest problem for me is, no matter where I go, I can't get away from myself."

Herb spoke up. "You know, Steve, we're a support group. We try to be here for each other. But, none of us are formally trained in trauma. That's what you're talking about. I know the first time I talked about my combat traumas in a group, a small group at that, there was a trained psychologist to guide me through it. Without her, I don't know what I would have done that first time."

Steve looked at Herb then at a few of the others. "I get it, guys. I don't want to lay my trash on any of you. But things can't get much worse for me. I know my time is coming, and I need to get things said. If not here, where? But, if this is not the place for such, I won't bother you gentlemen anymore."

"I could take you over to the PTSD clinic to see one of the shrinks there," said Doc. "I'll get you hooked up and maybe you could even see someone about getting a place to stay."

"Fellas, thanks for listening. I'm done here. You guys…" Steve's voice trailed off as he stood. He walked through the door and the guys watched as he headed for the exit.

"That dude is fucked up," said Rabbit. "He's talking about the end coming and all that shit. He's gonna off hisself. I'll go fetch him back here."

"Then what are we going to do, Rabbit. We're not pros and we really can't force him to go to the clinic," said Herb.

"Yeah," Rabbit responded, "but we sure can't let him do what he's thinking 'bout." With this, Rabbit left to catch up with Steve. He returned in a couple of minutes out of breath.

"I didn't get to him. I saw some ol' beater haul ass out the parking lot. That musta been him. No way I was gonna catch him."

"I'll contact Dr. Djardin to see what, if anything, can or should be done," said Herb. "I'll let you guys know what he says."

Don spoke up. "Look, guys, this is the second time he's bailed on us. I think we get back to taking care of our own business. We, at least, want to be here. 'Nuff said." His comments reflected the feelings of at least half the guys.

With that, Boys Club adjourned. The boys were less chatty than usual as they made their ways to the parking lot.

It had been at least two months since Steve's last appearance at Boys Club. No one had seen him around. During the final stages of their most recent meeting, Steve nonchalantly walked through the door. The members were surprised at his showing up and his general demeanor seemed noticeably different. He stood more erect and walked with purpose. However, before any member protestations could be voiced, he raised his hand to silence those about to speak, and said, "Look, men, I know I'm not supposed to be here. I checked out without giving you guys a chance. Just let me say what I got to say and you'll not have to deal with me again."

"And why should we do that, Steve-o," Don replied, grimly mocking Tresmer.

"You should listen, because once you've heard me out, you just might be glad you did. And, you won't forget it."

Doc stepped in. "Look, Steve, I can't speak for everyone, but I'm willing to give you a few minutes. And, for those wanting to leave now, I say just go. There's nothing keeping anyone here, just like always."

With those words Don made a racket getting up and shoving his chair back in. He huffed out the door leaving behind, "This is fucked up." Two others quietly followed.

With clear annoyance, Doc said, "You took the floor, Steve,

so now use it. Say what you came to say."

"Thanks, Doc, and thank you men for hearing me out. This might sound strange, but I'll say things as best I can remember." Tresmer paused and looked downward. "In a way, things seemed to have happened only yesterday, but it was fifty plus years ago, and I may get some of the particulars scrambled. You guys remember when I told you about the dust off chopper having more KIA than wounded, well pieces of me were in three of those goddamned body bags."

"Get the fuck out," exclaimed the other Herb. "At least be real, mister."

"This is what I remember, I promise. I was driving my one-one-three to Dau Tieng. Next thing I know I'm looking down at a giant crater and GIs throwing body bags onto a chopper. Next thing after that, I'm wandering around some town I don't know, some American town. Been doing that ever since."

"Bullshit," from someone in the back.

"I know it sounds phony. I'm telling it the best I can. I'm almost done. Just a few more minutes," Steve pleaded.

He then told them about the pregnant woman and children he killed while clearing that building. This took place only a few days before he and his buddies were annihilated on that road through the Michelin.

"I don't know why it's important for me to get this out. I don't know all the rules. That day with the woman and kids will never leave, I'm sure. To this day I even catch a glimpse of her every so often." Steve now sat and looked to the floor for at least thirty seconds. No one spoke nor interrupted his reverie.

"There's something else, guys. I never talked to Dr Kent; I just heard you guys talking about him. This gathering shone like a beacon to me. It guided me here. Again, I don't know why. There's lots of things you don't know just 'cause you're dead, believe me. I wouldn't doubt that others like me saw that light and have been here before me. I also sense, based upon something inside me, that I'm not the only one of my kind that could be a member of this group now."

Steve looked up but not directly at anyone. He then silently rose to his feet and said, "Thank you, brothers." He walked to the door, began to open it, appeared to think twice, looked back, and smiled at the group and then simply walked through the closed door as if it were not there.

The men were wide-eyed and began looking around at each other. Finally, Herb said, "Hey, guys, I'm not quite sure what just happened except that was a major mind fuck. But, I think we just keep doing what we've been doing, treat each other the same. Why wouldn't we? Maybe that place made us all ghosts in its own way."

Author's Comments:

There are two parts to this story: the combat action in Vietnam and the process of the ghost revealing himself to the support group. Likewise, my inspiration for this story is derived from these two situations that are separated by fifty years.

In the Vietnam War, I was assigned to the mechanized infantry unit that was portrayed clearing a village. Also, the daily log entry that concludes the first part of the story is the actual entry for my unit on February 28, 1970. I was on the armored personnel carrier that was blown up by the land mine. However, I jumped off the vehicle minutes before the mine detonated. Because there was confusion over who exactly perished, it was initially reported to the rear echelon of my unit that I was killed in action. Fortunately, this error was corrected before my family was notified. Besides the enormity of the explosion and the friends I lost, the thing I most vividly remember from that day is the unseen hand that guided me off the vehicle. I've had a lifetime to ponder why I was spared and able to live a full life when my buddies were denied. Much of my PTSD and survivor's guilt stems from this incident.

The inspiration from the second part of the story involves my Vietnam veterans support group, Boys Club. The members of my group served as the models for the characters in the story. I used their personalities and even their first names. I recall that during one of our discussions, we ruefully wondered how many of our memories have faded beyond our grasp. We admitted that it is for the best that some of these memories were lost. Having left parts of ourselves in Vietnam and having brought back PTSD is perhaps what contributes to each man's ghostliness.

Glossary of Terms:

The list that follows does not need to be read in its entirety to appreciate the story. However, there are terms in the story that may not be understood by all readers. This list should provide an understanding for those terms.

Moving On

III Corps (pronounced three core) – The US military split South Vietnam into regions called Corps. This was for combat command and administrative reasons. There were four Corps areas in South Vietnam beginning with I Corps in the north down to IV Corps in the southernmost part of the country.

grunt – infantry soldier who patrolled on foot.

mechanized infantry – infantry soldiers who patrolled on armored personnel carriers.

klick – kilometer

world – the United States

APC – armored personnel carrier (Army designation M113) was a vehicle soldiers rode while on patrol.

.50 cal – the M2 heavy machine gun. This was the most common weapon mounted on American APCs during the Vietnam war.

mortar track – An APC equipped with medium-sized mortars that could fire artillery-like projectiles several kilometers. The mortars were installed on the interior of the vehicle and fired through retracting doors in the roof.

fire mission – The soldiers would fire mortars at a specified target.

hooches – small buildings, often mere shacks.

bandoliers – ammunition carriers that soldiers usually wore crisscross around their upper torsos.

M-16 – the primary weapon soldiers carried in the Vietnam War.

Number 10 cans – three quart food cans that the Vietnamese often scavenged from US military dumps.

newbie or FNG – American soldiers newly arrived for duty in Vietnam.

25th Division – the 25th Infantry Division, a unit that consisted of approximately 12,000 soldiers. These were front line troops that carried out combat operations against enemy forces.

Dau Tieng – an American base camp. Base camps usually consisted of a number of battalion sized units; battalions were manned by 1000 to 1200 soldiers. These base camps served as the home base for combat units as well as the base for logistical operations in a given area.

lager – the defensive position a mechanized infantry unit would assume. It consisted of a number of APCs (and their machine guns) facing outward and often had fighting positions between the APCs. Think of wagon trains that circled up at night.

Michelin Plantation – the France-based Michelin rubber company's plantations that usually consisted of thousands of rubber trees.

Bobcats – the nickname officially given to soldiers of the 1st Battalion 5th Infantry Regiment (Mechanized) of the 25th Infantry Division.

Tay Ninh – an American base camp

dusted off – medically evacuated (medevaced) from the field by helicopter.

_M 548_ – a supply version of APC

final drive – the transmission of an APC or M548

DAV – Disabled American Veterans: a service organization established to support veterans.

Visitings

by James Henry Taylor

On a commonplace afternoon late in the fall, Brody walked into his house from the attached garage, having returned from teaching at the local university. As soon as he'd closed the door behind him, he detected a faint whiff of cat piss. He sniffed again; it was still there, not some momentary olfactory illusion. Kitty Kit had been adopted out to a permanent home over two years before, so it struck him as odd that it was only appearing for the first time. Had it been released by a specific combination of temperature and humidity? Or was it something that only seemed to smell like cat urine?

He climbed the two short sets of stairs to the main floor, using his nose only occasionally so it wouldn't become deadened to the scent. The most logical place to look for the source was the room where he'd kept the litter box—a space lined by bookcases filled with records, books, and CD's; and small, unmatched tables displaying odd toys, found objects, and other memorabilia. Brody got on his knees and put his face just above the center of the small Persian rug where the cat box had been. A few deep breaths through his nostrils produced only the smell of carpet.

He left the room and wandered around the house, picking

up a hint here and there that quickly faded to nothingness. Shrugging his eyebrows and twisting his mouth, he finally gave up.

Until early the following spring, he'd notice the same smell every few days or so. But he could never figure out what was causing it, where it was coming from, or why it was so unpredictable. Eventually, it disappeared for good.

It must have been about two or three in the morning, a time when he would typically awaken to go to the bathroom or get a glass of water, generally both. Brody opened his eyes and saw two figures the size of boys about eight or nine years old start to dash into the room. The pair froze in position, backlit faintly by the glow from the nightlight in the bathroom off the hall. They seemed to be made from—not dressed in— scraps and tatters of Confederate flags. Wheeling and tumbling over themselves, they frantically darted back down the hall.

He assumed it was another one of the "visions" he'd been having for the last year or so: unaccountable things, though not always particularly strange. Once a glittering net falling from the ceiling; another time, a swirl of winking stars below the ceiling fan. Always there as he first opened his eyes from sleep, and usually banished with a few blinks.

Brody pushed back the bedclothes, went to the toilet, got himself a drink of water, and returned to bed. "That one will be worth writing down," he thought as he pulled the covers over his shoulder and up to his chin. Part of his little collection to be: dreams, and half-dreams seen on the point of waking.

He hadn't fallen asleep yet, which wasn't surprising since

he hadn't been lying in bed more than ten or fifteen minutes. For no special reason, Brody opened his eyes. The room across the hall, where the litter box had once been, was very dark, yet there was enough almost-light from the shaded window that he could make out the shape of the largest bookcase. Standing in front of it, slightly to the right of center, was a dark-skinned figure of a man, somewhere between six and seven feet tall, he guessed. It wore a pale loincloth, and its face was painted in imitation of a skull. White slashes on the chest, arms, and legs indicated the other major bones.

Brody closed his eyes. "Here we go again." But he couldn't resist opening them several seconds later. The figure was where it had been, facing him, arms hanging by its sides, unmoving. Brody closed his eyes and rolled over, but a minute or two later he rolled back and looked once more. The skeleton-man was still there.

"Your eyes are playing tricks," he told himself. "It's too dark in there to really make out much of anything, and your mind's just filling in the blanks. You know there's really nothing there.

"And you're not getting up to make sure."

Close to dawn, with a faint light filtering through the bathroom curtains and leaking around the shade covering the window by the bed. When Brody's eyelids opened, a scrawny, dry-skinned, white-haired woman was standing close by. Her hair was pulled back—except for a few stray wisps—and she wore a shiny scarlet bathrobe over pale pajamas. Leaning forward slightly and shaking her right index finger at him, she seemed like a scolding schoolteacher. But a silent one, like every visitor before her.

"I've had enough of this," Brody felt, and whisked the

back of his hand at her a couple of times, consigning her to the void, the way a medieval prince might have sent away a disappointing servant.

She quickly dissolved from view, and he rose to go to the bathroom. When he looked toward the window, he thought, "Might as well just get up."

◊ ◊ ◊

"He saw me that night, of that I am sure. Three times, he faced me with open eyes. But he never showed any other sign."

"He saw us, too, he must have, but he just laid there like we was nothin'. Di'n't yell or jump up or come after us or nothin'. Like he di'n't care. Like he di'n't believe we was there."

"Yeah, like he thought we was nothin'. Damn Yankee."

"Yeah, damn Yankee. Bet he's one o' them atheists, too."

"Perhaps, perhaps . . ."

"Well, I must say I definitely did not appreciate the way he just lay there and waved his hand at me. 'Go away, old woman, go away.' Phoo! So disrespectful, as though he were merely shooing a fly."

"Meow!"

"That was not quite the same. He was never able to see you."

"Meow meow!"

"I meant no insult. We all know you are strong. And after all, you were the first among us to try to make him know we are here. That we still live in this place, a part of this piece of land.

"But the question we must ask ourselves now is: who

among all the others will visit him next?"

Author's Comments:

This story is based on real events (at least, as I experienced them). Only the final "explanation" is fictional (at least, I think it is).

Loving Ghosts
by R.M. Kinder

From the time I first heard of ghosts, I believed in them. My mother described knowing when her dear brother died, the exact time, probably, that he was killed by a bomb. She was awakened in the dark hours by the sense of someone near and heard the old wooden floor creaking with footsteps. Moonlight through the window fell a straight beam across the floor where no one walked. But the footsteps came from there, with pauses, too, as though some person stopped near her bed, looking down, maybe speaking. A farewell. My mother uses words like farewell, sweetheart, dearest one. He was her oldest brother, greatly loved, even as she grew older. Always handsome, always whole.

That's why ghosts are so vital—I mean the truth of them, that they exist, that they are around us, and that we will each become one. I suppose—know, I know!—that angels exist, and that they are of highest place. In the hierarchy of beings, they are next to God and his wife and son. But I don't know of angels as I do of ghosts, not internally, heartfelt—another of my mother's words. I suspect that beings grow into other beings, as caterpillars into butterflies. Thus ghosts may become angels, or an in-between something.

Loving Ghosts

I live in Buxton, a very small town in the state of Missouri, the United States of America. It's filled with ghosts, because cemeteries surround the town and are up in the hills near Delta and Cape, in the Old Fields, down in the Bootheel. I've gone out at night ever since I was truly young, six or so, and tried to see the fleeting of them, just wisps. The mist and fog that roll through here can trick the eye, but ghosts have a body to them. Though they can walk through objects—not always— and float, and maybe even make one part of themselves more visible than the others, they're a whole creature. A ghost can't divide itself. So the mist will be more together, longer or squatter, but together. I could see them. I didn't get in the way, or talk to them, but I didn't hide much either. I think a person can tell if a ghost is a mean one, out to do harm. I don't mean the pranksters. We know about them. They're petty mischiefs, perform little nasty acts, little meannesses, little griefs. They'll hide a letter or drip water on a line or two, so to make it unreadable.

One ghost is a soldier. Not my mother's brother. An older soldier. He came near me one night when I was down by the creek running behind our house. The moonlight shone on the water, and it rippled and the mist swirled across and up and sort of held upright near the tree a few feet away. Parts of it flowed off, like ghost water falling from the person. I heard music. It was real sweet, though high. A pipe, I think. Maybe a flute. I have a friend who plays a flute very well, not quite as sweetly, but the tone is close, soft and round. The ghost was a soldier, all right, and had played that kind of music and in that war. I guess it was the Civil War. I don't know if he was from the south or north. We in Missouri were both, and the war still continues, or so some of my relatives say. I would like that ghost, as he likes me. I think his name is Stephen. He's young.

I still live in my mother's house, but I have my own bank account, and I pay a part of our expenses. I've avoided the factory by being handy and willing to work. In a community as small as this, the jobs that really pay are passed around among the same families and their friends. I stay with people who are recovering from an illness or succumbing to one. I can clean, cook, preserve, garden, repair and varnish some old piece, set a new seat in a faucet or rewire an old lamp, if it's not too convoluted and if the owner will pay for the proper parts. I hate making do or jerry-rigging. That's another pejorative term of my mother's. A word of bias. The jerries were, my grandmother said, Germans. There's always a word for a person who's not of your country or your town or your family. It may be that angels and ghosts are also divided thus. Still, I would take a ghost rank.

I've wondered if there are female angels but I know the names only of the males mentioned in the standard Bible. I'm certain there are female angels in the history and presence of other peoples, those not in my culture. Maybe their angels are our demons.

Ghosts have gender. I think they still love what they loved while living, as my mother's brother loved her. When I stayed with Mrs. Lathan, who was dying at home and her daughter needed time for herself—time to forget grieving and burdens and regain compassion—I saw Mr. Lathan, who had died years before, maybe fifteen years. I was in the bedroom they had shared. Mrs. Lathan was barely there, taking the slightest breath, her chest not even rising, and her body making only a gentle slope in the covers. The room's light came from a copper lamp atop the sewing machine cabinet. The lamp shade had tiny cutouts so light flowed from the bottom and top but also in muted, blending streams from the shade. The light was ever moving over the rocking chair near the cabinet. I saw, without staring, that a form other than light was in the chair. I nodded a bit as recognition and greeting and in a few minutes I could see it was a man, dressed in a crumpled suit, with a pale shirt and a loosened tie. He had a thin face, and thin hair with some curl to it. There was a sweetness in the room. Not a scent. A feeling, like a dear warmth. My mother pronounces that word as warm-eth, which I like and have adopted. Mr. Lathan was visiting his wife. He was in the chair for a while, then gone, then I saw what must have been him in the rolling light near the bed. I believe he kissed her. Some kind, loving touch occurred. I felt the comfort of it in the room.

I'm glad I feel these things, but I feel lonely, too. None is kin to me that I know of. My mother has taught me not to talk about them, and to respect boundaries, never to call out a ghost.

Mrs. Lathan died Monday, and tomorrow is her funeral. My mother will go and I'll go, too. Many people will. She was a good woman. When Mrs. Lathan was newly widowed and still a heavy woman, my mother would send me early Sunday mornings to help her dress. She wore a corset, probably the only woman in our town who did so, and I had to lace it tight, which her husband had always done, and put the other layers on smoothly, buttoned or zipped. All adjustments created puffs of powder, which dusted my hair and clothing and made me sneeze. She was from another world, my mother said. The old one, where life was slower and things lasted, and people had rules about noise, and dress, and courtesy, and bravery. Now nothing is reliable except your own self and the people you're around long enough to learn and trust.

The service is in the small Church of Christ building, one room with the rear built up for a pulpit in front and a baptistry behind. A very plain church of very poor people. The pews are filled and the side aisle, too, with folding chairs borrowed from someone, maybe another church. In some things, churches cooperate. They're all working toward Heaven, Mother says, but with different criteria as to methods. There are high churches and low. Buxton has many of the latter.

In a loose file with other guests, we walk to the open casket, pause. My mother lays her right hand over Mrs. Lathan's hands. I feel my mother's emotions in my throat and eyes. It must be love of her because I'm sure I don't love Mrs. Lathan, though I like her. When we walk on, up the side aisle, I look around for the ghost of Mr. or Mrs. Lathan, who might want to gaze on old friends or to say farewell to the former self. There's no ghost. Maybe they feel unwelcome inside. The pews fill, and the elders of the church bring in folding chairs from someone's truck. Most of the elders are old, and in somber clothes. Not everyone wears dark colors, though Mother does and I do, to honor the deceased. In some communities, people have parties—food, music, and dance—to celebrate a life, the joy of life, but that's not the way in Buxton. I hope Mr. and Mrs. Lathan are somewhere much better, richer, glowing. Maybe they're dancing.

Mother and I are among the few who follow the hearse to the grave site. No one should be lowered in a grave without someone dear to throw the first soil onto the casket and to bow during the prayer. Mrs. Lathan has a good group, and the weather is warm, yet crisp, too. Leaves flitter over graves, pile by headstones, and edge vases. Fall now but winter coming. I move away from the guests who are saying farewell in slow ways. I stroll over to the Confederate Cemetery. Headstones face the east, so I walk north to south, reading names and turning completely around slowly, to spy any sign of ghosts. Though why would they stay here? To watch over the remains of others? Taking turns as sentinels? Or new ghosts, unsure where to go, or unwilling? Down the slope east, toward the trees lining the creek below, the air ripples like sun on moisture. And closer to me, maybe three yards behind, a haziness. I blink my eyes and it is beside me, like light sparkles when you try to see the sun. Taller than I. Then another comes and another. I feel their presence, a fluidity and slight pressure.

My mother waves me toward her, come, time to leave, and she turns away with the others, heading toward the cars. The ghosts are still here, a bit apart from one another, allowing me passage. When I am a few feet away and peer back, I see one has accompanied me, the taller one. "I'm Naomi," I whisper. In the next few seconds I feel a chill and know the ghost isn't the one I sought.

Mother waits for me by the car, her chiding expression a warning. "Did you see something?"

"No." It's true in a way. I didn't see them, only the presence of them.

The grave will not be filled in until we leave, for which I, and probably most of the others, are grateful. I know it's not the end.

"Come get in the car, Naomi. Don't gather anyone in."

I could invite the ghosts with a glance and maybe with only a thought. But I won't act against my mother's wishes. She chose long ago not to see them. She had prayed to have no ability. She believes that thinking of the next life weakens both responsibility and joy in this one. "What if you belong in neither," I asked her. She said that wasn't possible.

I go to bed early, thinking my mother might do the same, but she keeps the television low which means she is reading or working puzzles and the voices are nonintrusive company. I try thinking Stephen near and suddenly feel alert, successful, not alone. He is outside, near the west window of my bedroom, beneath the linden tree. I want to join him but my mother, though quiet, is still in the living room. I dwell only on Stephen, the ghost who plays the flute, and I hear it, faint, that music of his. I know the melody a little now, and listen closely. A sweet tune, Stephen's song.

I wake, into total dark, but someone is at the foot of my bed. Not Stephen. I sense him more than see him. The darkness there is thicker. I stay quiet and unmoving. When I was a child, there used to be two of them, hooded. They never spoke. They accompanied the twilight of my sleep, when the body is immobile and must stay that way until, capable of springing away or screaming, it wakes, and the shadow forms flee. I was afraid of them.

Morning again, and my mother goes to the factory where she sews pockets onto men's trousers. She's so quick and her stitches are perfect, straight when needed, curved gently around corners, no dangling loops or tiny crumples. She hums, even though fast music pumps high and loud, so the workers can't talk, pass joke or prayers. They have their ways. Mother tells me some of the sexual pranks hidden in stacks of pockets or pant legs. She won't laugh aloud, but covers her mouth and turns her head while her shoulders shake. She likes a good joke and will pass it to me, but not condone it fully. I think she loved my father and was very physical with him. I know I'm physical though I have yet to be kissed as a grown girl should be. As I dream it. With lips only partly open, warm, pressing against my own.

Ruthie, my best friend since grade school, lives on this same street, only three blocks north, past small houses like ours and three huge ones passed down by old money, and on one side a laundromat and on the other a store converted from a small house where a single lady died of bone cancer. People took turns caring for her. She didn't have money and we're a kind town.

Ruthie is my age and soon will be off to live in the northwest with her older sister. She's been working in the same factory as my mother. She wants to escape, to leave Buxton forever. And she wants me to come. We could find work and find a place to live and fall in love with a cowboy. She has her heart set on that. She will learn to ride a horse and to cut a calf from a herd and all sorts of cowboy mysteries.

"You should go with her if she really wants you to," my mother says. "You girls have always helped each other."

"I want to stay here, Mom. I can get my own place any time you want, if that's the problem."

"No," she says. "That's not the problem. Your happiness is."

She doesn't want to believe that what makes me happy is what I have.

I sing the flute song with syllables, softly, while Ruthie holds her flute ready and nods her head. It's a waltz, da da da, da da da, da da da, da … … da da da, da da da, da da da, da … … da da da, da da da, da da da … … da da da, da da da, da da da, da… Twice more and Ruthie plays it alone. She's very good! The sound blooms around us, floats away.

"That's it," I tell her. "Exactly. You played it closer than I could sing it."

"I learned it from you."

I hadn't thought of this as teaching. "Don't give me the credit. It's your talent."

"Some patterns are easy and I don't have to think about it. The music leads to it. I'd like to hear the whole piece."

"So would I. I only know a part."

Ruthie is very small and lovely, black, black hair, cut shoulder length and a little wavy, her skin very pale, and eyes light blue. Mother says Ruthie's striking. She's very delicate, actually frail, and often slowed down by breathing problems. Sometimes I hear my own breathing and it makes me anxious. No one should have to think about breathing, but Ruthie does.

Ruthie thinks the music comes from somewhere in the neighborhood, through an open window in the houses across the creek.

"No," I say. "It seems to come down. Sort of falls."

She gives me her "I see" look, head cocked and eyelids partly lowered. "I'd like to hear that." Then, "Tell me the rest of it, Naomi."

I want to tell her, not everything, but about a few ghosts she might already have seen without knowing it, like the white rippling on the porch swing of Carol Walford's house, and the same rippling at school in the back of the room. Mrs. Fields wondered who of us had written "Goodbye" on Carol's folder. "I hope you meant a kindness," she said, studying our faces. Only a few times have I seen the true features, like Carol, Mr. Lathan, and Jimmy Turman's sister.

"I see ghosts."

The backyard glows in moonlight, ringed in shadows that

are in daytime trees and bushes, as if the town doesn't surround us now. I wish I had kept this sliver of life to myself. I wonder if my mother sees my father and doesn't say so, to keep him. If Mrs. Lathan spoke to the old gentleman every day of her life even when his ended. Maybe everyone can see ghosts but dares not tell. I told.

Ruthie cuts diagonally from the sidewalk, flute in hand, no case. She's wearing a white dress with a full skirt, and black slippers. She looks like a child angel but her steps rattle the bits of gravel where we had a driveway.

"You didn't tell me how to dress," she says.

"Like me," I whisper, and she gives a little smile. We've never dressed alike. I motion her to follow me.

Moonlight slides over the trees scattered along the creek, drips down to the undergrowth and shallow water. There's no place for her to sit.

"What now?" she asks.

"Listen. Look."

"For what? The mist? A ripple?"

"Are you making fun?"

"No. Sorry." She holds up the flute. "Should I begin?"

"Not yet."

There's no true silence, but millions of faint sounds of different lengths and tones, like dots and curls and beats and strings. The sounds of light and dark and everything within them. The night opens and closes and life comes and goes. Streams.

"Naomi," Ruthie says, "don't close your eyes."

She's my best friend and has always been. She's frail-bodied but a strong person. "You can play now," I say. "A couple times through, and then be quiet again. All right?"

She nods, brings the flute to her lips, but can't steady the flute where she wants it, and when she does begin, her forced breath creates a hollow whistle from the mouthpiece. She moistens her lips, rolls them together, and positions them again. In a few seconds, the music emerges, high, but sweet and round. It's lovely. It's like her, who she is in another form. Gentle. When she stops and lowers the flute, her pale face is expectant. She's listening for Stephen. Then her eyes dart to me, away, her lips part. I see she hears it, is caught in the wonder of it. I strain to hear. I look for signs of him. She begins playing again, a different tune, lower, long notes. Sad.

She stops. "I think he's gone," she whispers. "Has he?"

"I think so. When you talk, Ruthie, I can't listen."

"Sorry. But that wasn't the tune you taught me. Has he played that before?"

"I don't know. I didn't hear anything except you."

"You're teasing me. You didn't hear it? That flute?"

"No."

"Why not? That doesn't make sense. You believe me, though, don't you?" She peers down the upper bank in both directions. "I'm afraid, Naomi. I don't think I should have done this."

"Nothing's going to happen. Maybe just one person can hear it at a time."

"Well, I don't want to be the one. I thought we'd be listening together, you know? Now I feel like this wasn't a good idea. Not for me. I really am afraid."

I don't know what I've done. "I wanted to share something of mine before you left."

"I don't want it. I want to go home. We can talk later. Tomorrow."

"I'll walk you."

"No. Stay under the streetlight and watch me. I'll know you're there."

She runs a short distance, but stops, looks back and returns my wave, then walks. She can't breathe well enough to run. She turns twice more. When I can't see her, I know she is almost home but I remain at my station until she has to be in her house. I'm uncertain if she made it. I run down our junky sidewalk, past sleepy houses. At Ruthie's, I see her bedroom is lighted and I wait to see movement inside. I do, and relief flows through me. Why am I not in danger if Ruthie is? I will miss her so. I start home. The courthouse clock is visible the whole way, that top spire pointing up, up, up. I don't agree with it. Life is here, too, down and around. Our front door will be locked, so I have to enter through the rear of the house. I wait on the back steps for a while. I hear the night wind through leaves.

Ruthie phones me late morning. She wants to talk about last night, but uptown, in the long café that used to be the bus station and where we'd go after school each day for an hour or so. She asks me what does it mean that she heard music that I didn't hear. She wants to understand exactly what has happened. I see a wariness in her eyes and I do want to erase that. It's my doing. "I don't know what it means. I've only heard the one melody. But I've seen ghosts all my life, Ruthie, and nothing has ever happened to me. There's no substance."

"But I've heard something you didn't hear. So it's different. How can you be sure something isn't going to follow me?"

"Ghosts don't follow people." I remember my mother's brother, whose ghost crossed the ocean to say goodbye to her sleeping form. "Maybe loved ones. They stay close to where they died."

"How do you know?"

"It's the common lore about ghosts."

"So, whoever it is," Ruthie says, "he's at your house? And will stay there?"

I nod, though the creek belongs to the neighborhood. Maybe the ghost belongs to the neighborhood.

"Good. But I don't want you to have any trouble, either," she says.

Our sandwich and tea have come. Ruthie is easier now, talks of the belongings they've already shipped to Wyoming. I hold my half of the sandwich up ready to take a bite, but I can't. My lips are trembling, and Ruthie notices. "I know," she says. "I feel the same way. But I can't live here my whole life like my mother has. I have to get away."

Sonny McGee stops his tall self by our table, friendly and long talking, and sweet on Ruthie, and sometimes on me. He married one of our friends but flirting is his way, and almost everyone indulges him. Kind, homely guy. I take a bite of the sandwich while he's there, and manage to swallow it with sips of tea. Sonny closes his visit with one heavy hand on Ruthie's shoulder and one heavy hand on mine. Equally his favorite girls. He strolls off. Ruthie is still across from me, but she's already some distance away. The ribbon between us is fading and loosening.

"Maybe the ghost thing had to happen," she says. "To help us say goodbye."

The afternoon sunlight is that limpid late August one, like summer giving to fall though it's early for the season shift. Ruthie gets in her car and offers me a ride, but I want to walk. It's easier than stretching our loss down the road. The sidewalk goes the whole way home, except for intersecting narrow streets. One of the first corners is the funeral home. I deliberately search for any sign as I pass, though usually I drop my eyes on this corner, as I do on church corners. Instinct or reverence. Both probably. If there's a ghost here, it's ahead, at the edge of the lawn. Just a shimmer and leaves trembling on a nearby spirea. It could be a tiny dust devil, or a parasite in the leaves. Ruthie and I may never have been good friends, never have been truly close. As I pass the trembling, shining space I am compelled to speak, for whatever reason. "Good afternoon to you."

At home, my mother is resting from the day's work. I fix a simple supper, am drawn now and then to look down the expanse of back yard, with the shadow of our house taller and narrower at the top, like a collapsed building with turret. I have to see what's left to me and adjust my needs accordingly. There's no peace or happiness in longing for what isn't and never will be possible.

Mother asks about Ruthie and when they're leaving and if I would ever consider going to live in Wyoming or visit. It's good, she says, to have a friend close by when you begin a new venture. Moving to a new town can be very frightening. You begin with one friend and build a community.

"What if you don't have one friend?"

"Did something happen between you and Ruthie?"

"No. But her heart is sort of set on a different life, I can tell. She wants to start fresh."

"I doubt that's true, hon. You're just feeling hurt over something."

Yes, I am. Loss. Of Ruthie and of what I alone had.

After supper, twilight, I return to the place where Ruthie had played. I sit on a low stump, hug my knees close. The sun sinks, and a pale moonlit night descends. Then a thrum sounds, so low I think something huge and far away is moving and the earth trembles and that's what I hear. A groan. But it lifts and loosens and lightens. It's the melody Ruthie played, though deeper. I feel it in my lungs and my body. Such a sound. I keep my head down so I won't encounter any face, any sign, nor invite. The melody is clearer now, near, too, and something familiar about it puzzles me. Alarms me. What is it? I rise, and, despite my curiosity, walk toward my mother's house. As I pass by the kitchen window and then reach the corner and the back steps, and walk up them, I realize why the tune is familiar. I don't play music but I have an ear for it. This is Stephen's tune, but backwards, deeper and backwards.

So I know, for sure. I've invited something.

From sleep, I hear our phone ringing and my mother's footsteps quick in the hall and the ringing stops. It's very early, pearl light only at the upper rim of curtains.

"Naomi?" Mother says softly from the open doorway. "It's Ruthie. She needs to talk to you."

I'm up immediately. I know. I know.

"She sounds very upset," my mother says, her eyes worried, wondering a question at me. "I asked her what's wrong but she wants you."

"I'll tell you as soon as I know, Mom."

She watches as I pick up the phone, but I turn my back to her. "Ruthie? What is it?" In a few seconds my mother leaves me alone.

Ruthie heard the music last night, heard it outside from her bedroom. She peeked out the window and she swears there was someone there. He was tall and very dark, not skin dark, all dark, like a living shadow. "And that's not all," she says. "I want to tell you but not over the phone. Will you come down here? Right now?"

Of course I will. I slip on the jeans I wore yesterday and the same blue shirt. I button it unevenly, but that's no matter. My mother is now in my doorway.

"I'll make my bed later," I say. "I've got to help Ruthie for a minute."

"What is it? Are they okay?"

"Oh yes," I say. "She needs help moving something and she doesn't want to ask her mother. I don't mind."

"You sure that's all? She really sounded frightened."

"If it's anything more, I'll tell you when I get back."

Ruthie opens the door before I knock, gestures me in, across the living room to her bedroom. "I told Mom I had some photos and things to give you. We'll have a few minutes while she's having her coffee." A couple boxes are on her bed and the flute case is propped vertical in a wingback chair. Ruthie's room has two outer walls, each with a huge window, one south and one east. Soft light floods her room. She's been crying. Her eyes are puffy and the lashes damp and pointed. She sits on one side of the boxes, so I sit on the other. She hands me a stack of photos tied with a red ribbon. "These are for you."

"Tell me what happened."

"He was in the house. After I looked out, I got in bed and pulled the covers up. I didn't know what to do. I couldn't call the police. I wanted to call you. I didn't want to scare my mother. She's older than your mother. She could die."

"Did you see him in the house or hear him?"

"Saw him." She points past me. "Right there."

"At the foot of the bed?"

She nods. "Absolutely a real thing. Not a human person. I mean not a living person, but not a ghost, either. He was dark and sort of solid. Not a ghost."

"Could you see his face?"

"No. I saw his eyes and maybe his mouth. He had on a robe with the hood pulled up. It was a dark robe, with a rope around the waist. I want you to get him out of my house and my yard. Please. Can you do that?"

"I think so."

"Right now? Will you do it now?"

"You have to pray. My mother didn't want to see ghosts and she prayed about it. That stopped it. So you should pray for the same."

"I don't pray, Naomi. Nobody's going to listen to me."

"Yes, He will." I don't know this, but I want her to feel safe.

"You have to pray with me. I don't know what to say." She pushes the boxes away, kneels on the floor by the bed. I kneel by her side.

"I don't know how to start," she says.

"Say 'Dear Lord' or 'Dear Father in Heaven,' and then ask that the ability to see beyond this life be taken away from you and that He keep you safe from all harm."

"You say it with me."

"Then I would be praying for me."

"And you're not willing to do that? To give it up yourself?"

"I'll pray for you. I'll go first and you can follow my lead." I take her right hand in my left. "Dear Father, I come to you to ask that you take Ruthie under your wing, that you keep all harm from her in this life, that you forgive her for any wrongdoing and that you take from her any special knowledge that would frighten her or put her at risk for bodily or spiritual harm. I ask, Lord, that whatever threatens Ruthie, if it cannot be done away with, be given to me instead, so that she need not fear forever. In Your dear son's name, Amen."

Ruthie's hand tightens, squeezes mine. "Dear Father, I thank You for my friend Naomi and I ask that You listen to her prayer for me, and forgive me for being afraid of praying to You. Please keep us both safe. Please take from me whatever has followed me and whatever ability I have that makes it want me. In Your son's name. Amen."

We sit back. Ruthie's eyes are very open and moist, but not tearful. "Do you think it'll work?"

"Yes. It already has. You don't have to worry."

She stands up, offers her hand to help tug me up. Then she takes the flute case from the chair, holds it out to me. "I want you to take this."

"I can't play it."

"I don't want it anymore. I'm never going to play it again, even open the case."

"You can't give up music."

"No. But I can get another flute. If you don't want it, I'm going to throw it away. We're not taking it with us."

"You're afraid of it?"

She nods.

I want to tell her that the flute isn't the fault. I am the instrument. But I understand she has to feel that she has passed on the creature or closed his entrance to her life. We have prayed but prayer isn't an act Ruthie has faith in. Destroying or giving away makes more sense to her. Like washing her hands. "I'll take good care of it. If you ever want it back, it's yours."

"No. Don't say that. Say you'll accept it."

Already she's learned something I recognize as right. "I accept it."

"Okay. There." She runs her small fingers through her thick hair, combing it back from her face. "I wanted to give you something really good. Special. I had thought maybe the flute. Now …I guess it's ruined for both of us." She puts her hand over her heart, sniffs. She shouldn't cry. It makes breathing hard.

"No. It isn't ruined. I love the thought. And I'm so sorry I scared you."

"I'll get over it."

"You're going to be very happy," I say. "And cowboys will love you."

My mother waits in the living room. "Is that Ruthie's flute case?"

I raise the packet of photos. "Yes. She gave it to me, and this stack of pictures."

"So what's wrong?"

"Maybe homesickness already. She wanted to say goodbye." Those words lurch out of me.

"Why would she give you her flute?"

She follows me into my bedroom. I put the flute in the over-stuffed, wide-armed blue velvet chair that had in my childhood been in the living room, then displaced by a new one. I prop the flute case vertical as Ruthie had done. I know nothing about the proper way to leave an instrument at rest. "She plans to get a better one," I say. "I've always loved Ruthie's music. She thought I might want to learn how to play."

"That's sweet of her," Momma says, but with her arms folded across her midriff and looking at the flute. Her voice is thoughtful. When she turns to me, she's still questioning.

"Something's up with you girls."

"No more than usual. She's sad and afraid. Everything is going to be new for her."

Momma takes up the packet of pictures. "May I look at these?"

While she does, I gather a change of clothes to take to the bathroom. "I'm going to shower."

When I come into the kitchen, she's having coffee. The café curtains are open to the back yard and the early-risen sun. I get coffee, too, and join her at the table.

"Those pictures are all of you girls together. Just the two of you. Some of them are ones I took. Why would she give them to you? We probably have them."

"I don't know the answer to that, Momma."

"It's strange."

"Maybe she has copies in an album, or only wants to keep a few and doesn't want to toss the rest."

"You didn't ask?"

"I haven't looked at them yet. You took the ribbon off. You make too much of things."

She smiles, but her eyes are still troubled. "Maybe," she says, "but you're a serious child."

"I know. Ruthie and I are all right, and I'm going to be all right without her. I'm not like her. I'm not like you, either."

She bobs her head like she knows what I mean and there's no worry. We chat in the kitchen about little matters, how a heavy, covered butter dish keeps butter cool enough not to spoil, how her mother used to lower butter, milk, and sometimes other food down the cistern to keep them cool, how hard to keep squirrels from ruining many pecans to get a bite or two from each.

It's Saturday and we spend most of the day doing the ritual once-a-week cleaning. Even baseboards get a swift wipe-down this time, a once-a-month duty. Sometimes picture frames, sometimes books. My mother sets the inside tasks. All maintenance and outside work I do, like insulating pipes in winter, pruning, removing or planting a bush, disposing of dead mice or birds. Cleaning debris along the creek.

Across the creek is where Jimmy Turman's family lived. We were in third grade together, along with Ruthie and Sonny McGee. Jimmy and I used to play Tarzan. We'd swing on a low branch and drop down on the other side. One day we planned to kiss after school. He was going to meet me at the creek and give me a proper kiss. That was a sweet thought then, as now. We walked home together and then we split to reach our houses. He had to report in before playing. My mother was still at the factory. I went down to the creek and sat on the low, flat part of the bank, so I would appear dainty. The kiss happened just as it was supposed to. I watched him crossing the grassy lot to the bank opposite, saw his smile at me as he gripped the branch we'd been using, now supple. He dropped very near me. We didn't say anything. I think we shared the idea of kiss. He sat down, turning toward me, bracing himself with his left arm, so our shoulders touched, mine a bit inside his. He bent his head down and I leaned toward him and our lips touched and remained touching for a few seconds, at least. It was so warm, so sweet, so perfect. Then he leaned back and we talked about Mrs. Graham's harsh voice and how she liked to spank girls over her knees, which was very ugly. We didn't talk about getting married when we grew up or about being boyfriend girlfriend. And we didn't kiss again. We played Tarzan a few more afternoons, then the winter came.

Later, in junior high, his older sister died of meningitis, suddenly, like being at school on Friday and not alive on Sunday morning. When Jimmy came back to school and I saw him in the hall, I told him how sorry I was about his sister. It was a real tragedy. His face quickened with such sorrow that I nearly choked and I touched his hand and said, "She's not really gone. You'll see her again." He stared at me and I feared he'd draw away, but he didn't. He eased. "You think that's true?" With all my heart I said, "I know it is." He nodded twice. "Okay, then. Okay." He walked off, wiping his face. He wore a blue-and-white checkered shirt, jeans. He had thick brown hair, home-cut. I could see his sister. She went down the stairs a step or two behind him. She was his height and weight, wearing jeans and sandals. Her long hair was in one thick rope braid. Her image was wavery, like through warm air or shallow water. She didn't want to leave her brother. He later married a girl named Frances who had been a friend of his sister's. I was so happy to have helped him not hurt.

I don't know if I saw Jimmy's sister because I said she still existed or simply because she does. I don't know if Mr. Lathan became accustomed to me or if I became aware of him. If my beliefs and hopes spring into being, then the dark visitors are mine too and what I say or think of them or open to them is mine, no matter how disastrous that might be. I could pray that I not be able to see them, but suppose I do. Prayer is itself an act. I will have denied a gift and disowned a part of myself. I want the role in life that is mine. I'm between two worlds. I don't know the maker of them, or His intentions, but I know where I belong, and I'm happy and willing to stay.

When my mother goes to bed, I look at the photos Ruthie gave me. I am much larger than Ruthie, and very fair, soft looking. My image appears not blurred but almost outlined, as if the air closest to me is darker. I rub at that outline in each photo and study each beneath the lamp shade. Is it truly there? Ruthie chose these photos for me. She saw it. I tie the ribbon around them, put them in the dresser drawer. I am very lonely this moment, heartsick, but that's all right. I am becoming. So is Ruthie. We will be what we will be. Everywhere, all over the world, people say hello, say goodbye. Never for the last time. They linger and long and love.

I leave my mother's house, move out into the night. I hum that sweet tune, breaking it into syllables, tiny sounds. I hum. I listen.

Author's Comments:

The major inspiration for this story is the vast number of accounts from individuals who have had extrasensory experiences or shared in them. Research has led me to know about the possible physiological reasons for some of the experiences. The hooded beings, for example, that Naomi sees in her bedroom, are common to people who have sleep paralysis. While still unable to move in deep sleep, the mind wakens. That experience can be prompted by a medical procedure that stimulates a certain part of the brain. But as one researcher noted, the fact that the vision can be stimulated by prodding doesn't mean that's the only stimulus. John Geiger's book, *The Third Man Factor*, was also an inspiration. He reports and discusses the accounts given by over a hundred near-death survivors about a helper that appeared in dire times to guide or comfort them. Again, there are physiological reasons why this might occur, and why that feeling might lead to clearer thinking, sharper vision, and added strength. In times of extreme stress, the mind switches to the primitive brain. Since people who are not under stress, or near death, and do not suffer sleep paralysis also have these experiences, I've come to the belief that there are forces in us or around us that guide and protect—and other forces that threaten and mislead.

FIN

by Chuck Hocter

Often touted as the shortest horror story in the world:
"The last man on Earth sat alone in a room. Suddenly, there was a knock on the door."

Harold Eugene Watson, the last—or so he supposed—man on Earth, sat alone in the living room of his home. He was pondering whether he should get up and fix some lunch or just sit and stare at his dead, blank 85 inch TV, dead because there was no longer any power to operate it. There didn't seem to be any power to operate anything anymore. None of his state-of-the-art appliances worked. His car didn't work. His computer didn't work. The list of things that didn't work seemed to stretch from his living room to infinity and beyond, to quote a popular toy from a few years ago, which if he had one, probably wouldn't work either.

It had all started innocently enough. Some idiots had naively assumed they could change the totalitarian government next door by crossing the border and staging a protest. They figured all their oppressed brethren would join in and the bad men would surrender power and all would be sunshine, lollipops, and roses. Well, of course, the bad men didn't. Instead, they rounded up all the intruders, stood them up in the capitol city square and executed them on live TV. Naturally, this act sparked near-universal condemnation. And as these things sometimes go, someone fired a shot, someone blew up a building, someone dropped a bomb, someone else dropped a bigger bomb, and so on, and so on. EMP's took out technology. Radiation, disease, and starvation took out the people. Only those living in near complete isolation, in the far backwaters of the world, survived the initial onslaught. Despair took a few more survivors out. Petty arguments settled by readily available firearms took many more. Ignorance of the basic skills necessary for day-to-day existence killed off some. Attrition was rapid, like a snowball rolling downhill. As the population declined, rumors sprang up of "others," as in "not human" walking among the remnants of humanity, slaughtering and devouring and engorging themselves on their terror. Some said they were aliens, disgusting in form and habits. Others swore they were physical manifestations of nightmares and ancient legends come back to facilitate the demise of the human race. Regardless, the population kept dwindling till it was down to Harold Eugene Watson—and one other.

The last man on Earth sat alone in a room. Suddenly, there was a knock at the door. Harold heaved his not inconsiderable bulk up and out of his recliner and schlumped to the door. He swung it open to reveal the ever smiling face of his next door (as in five miles down the road) neighbor, Sallyanne Benedict. Harold had once considered courting Ms. Benedict but found her unflinching cheerfulness unbearable. He had always been the kind of person who just needed a little gloom and doom in his life, not that there was any lack of said conditions these days. But Sallyanne ignored the irrefutable fact of the existence of the apocalypse and toddled merrily on her way. Strangely, she hadn't toddled his way in over a week. She was usually good for an appearance every couple of days.

"Harold, dear, do you happen to have any molasses? I'm baking some cookies and just discovered that I'm completely out. I would drive into town but for some reason my car won't start and I don't feel up to riding my bicycle sixty miles into town to get some. You know, we used to have a grocery truck come around once a week and he carried all sorts of commodities and he was the nicest man. Mr. Antonucci was his name. He had a funny little accent and always tipped his hat to the ladies. Of course this was before you came here. Then one week he just stopped coming. I wonder whatever became of him."

Without saying a word, Harold walked to the kitchen, found a jar of molasses way back on one of the shelves and brought it to her.

"Well, I must say, Harold, that you are still a man of few words. That's one of the things I've always admired about you. You're not one of those people that run on and on so no one else can get a word in edgewise. This jar looks a bit old. Has it been on the shelf long? Oh well, I suppose if I put it in some warm water the molasses will liquefy and be just as good as new. I have to run now or I'll never get those cookies baked so I can't sit and visit a while. Goodbye and, if you should develop a craving for some sweets, they should be done in an hour or two, so please stop by and sample a few. See you later?"

Harold smiled a sickly little smile, mumbled something incomprehensible, and gave a vague little wave as he shut the door behind her retreating figure. When he was sure that she had gone and he was once more alone, he loosed one explosive expletive, rolled his eyes toward the ceiling, and returned to his recliner and his staring at the dead TV.

A noise from outside startled Harold into wakefulness. He noted the gathering dusk and calculated that he had slept for at least three hours. His circadian rhythm was getting further and further out of whack. Before too long, he would be living like a vampire—up all night and sleep all day. Not that it mattered. He arose and went to the door, retrieving a flashlight from a desk drawer on the way. A sweep of the front yard area flushed out a coyote which ran off down the road in the direction of Ms. Benedict's. Had it been any other woman, Harold might have worried about her safety. But this one kept a thirty-ought-six rifle and a forty-five automatic pistol handy. Mr. Coyote might be in for a big surprise.

Feeling a bit peckish, Harold fixed himself a PBJ, noting that he would soon have to bake another loaf of bread—thank goodness for gas stoves. He finished his sandwich, downed a glass of warm grape juice and shuffled off to bed. He slept badly. Recurring flashes of the coyote and Ms. Benedict and a jar of molasses swirled around in his brain. Sometimes coyote would be licking the contents of the open jar, and other times Sallyanne would be sticking her finger into the jar and licking off the molasses. Finally, giving up on the idea of sleep, Harold got up, took a sponge bath with well water and fixed himself some breakfast. As he fried up some potatoes and Spam, he thought longingly of eggs over easy, sausage or even cereal and milk, but lack of refrigeration had put an end to those delicacies. He finished his breakfast and tidied up the kitchen—one shouldn't live like a slob just because there wasn't anyone around to condemn one for it.

Remembering the coyote from last evening, Harold went

outside just as the sun was coming up, to check for tracks. He found them easily in the perpetual desert dust along with the two sets of footprints, coming and going, of Sallyanne. He followed them down the road for about a quarter mile where he came upon a most curious scene recorded in the dust. The tracks he'd been following were joined by another set of coyote tracks coming in from the north. Apparently, there had been a struggle between the coyote and Ms. Benedict. Then her footprints veered south toward the rather deep ditch at the side of the road, accompanied by what appeared to be parallel drag marks. A second set of footprints set off at an angle from the ditch heading west toward the Benedict homestead. Curious, Harold walked over and peered down into the dry ditch. There at the bottom, covered in dust, clothing disheveled, head and neck at an unnatural angle and staring up at the cloudless sky, lay Ms. Sallyanne Benedict.

Time passed slowly as Harold stood there contemplating the loss of the only other human known to have survived the apocalypse. She had been a thorn in his side, true, but she had also been an assurance that he was not alone in the vast uncertainty of the world as it now was. As he stood there, another chilling thought crept into his brain. Who had done this? He studied the tracks leading away from the ditch. They were identical to the ones he had followed here from his house, i.e. Sallyanne's. So, if she was dead in the ditch, who was filling her shoes and headed for her house?

Harold knew what he had to do but he knew that he would need some things from his house first. He went home. He took the 9mm automatic from his night stand, put it in the holster from a dresser drawer and strapped it on. He'd been living alone in the desert for the last five years and had become quite adept at shooting the heads off of rattlesnakes. Next he collected his rifle from the hall closet. It was a souvenir of his military training—an M-1 30 caliber carbine. It wouldn't bring down an elk but was effective on anything man-sized or smaller. Also it had a 30 round magazine, which might come in handy. Finally, he put on his aviator sunglasses and topped it all off with his old campaign hat from a war best forgotten. He looked in a mirror and had to laugh. He looked ridiculous—overweight, three-day-beard, rumpled clothes and lethal weapons—a study in contradiction.

Harold certainly wasn't going to march the five miles to Sallyanne's house. His 4x4 was useless. Any vehicle with a computer chip in it was dead, dead, dead. Fortunately, he was the proud owner of an old Johnny Popper John Deere tractor. It was a bear to start but once you got it going, it could make 10-15 mph in road gear and the digital revolution had come along decades after its manufacture. It only took three tries to get the green machine going and Harold was on his way.

The drive to Sallyanne's gave the reluctant hero time to think. He remembered the rumors of aliens and mythological beings on the loose. He'd written them off to hysteria or too much self-medicating against it all. But one local legend had fascinated him ever since he had moved here to the southwest. It was the Navajo belief in skinwalkers, spirits that could take the shape of animals, particularly the coyote. Presumably, they could also take the shape of humans. As he bounced along down the road, he took stock of his weapons and wondered what good, if any, they would be against a spirit. About halfway to his destination, Harold stopped. After a few minutes of deep contemplation, he put the old John Deere in gear, cranked the steering wheel hard right and released the clutch while standing on the right wheel brake. The green machine made a tight "U" turn and headed back toward home. Harold had decided that he was not as brave as the situation called for.

On reaching his home and putting the old tractor back in the barn, Harold divested himself of firearms, hat and shades, grabbed a fifth of Crown Royal from the cupboard and retired to his favorite spot, in his recliner in front of his regrettably dead TV. He had decided that some self-medicating of his own was in order.

The last man on Earth sat alone in a room. Suddenly, there was a knock on the door.

FIN

Author's Comments:

I have always loved the premise of the shortest horror story in the world. I threw in some Native American mythology to add to the post-apocalyptic flavor—and some molasses.

The Unkindest Cut
by James Henry Taylor

"YOU'VE NEVER SEEN ANYTHING LIKE IT!!!"

Well, that wasn't quite true. Art Barker's Wonder Hut actually housed the usual assortment of second-rate oddities: a meteorite the size of a child's fist; a chunk of fossilized dinosaur crap; Lola the dancing chicken (performances at 10, 12, 2, and 4); a blurry photograph of the ghost of Thomas Edison, a glowing light bulb in his outstretched hand; the preserved remains of a two-headed snake, a two-headed rat, a two-headed mole, etc., etc., etc.

Art displayed his collection in an eighty-foot long Quonset hut adorned with wide vertical stripes of blue and orange. The building was vintage WWII, bought from the Navy by Art's grandfather back in the early 50's. First it had been a machine shop, becoming a storage shed after old Henry passed away, and finally undergoing a magical 70's transformation into the Wonder Hut. This local version of Ripley's Believe-It-Or-Not had been Art's brainchild, back when he'd had a scraggly beard and reddish-blonde hair reaching slightly past his shoulders. "Indulgence" had been the watchword in those days, even among some small-town folk, so Art's parents had indulged him, letting him set up his museum next door to the real family business, Betty's U-Turn Café. (Betty Says: "IF U-WANT GOOD EATS, U-TURN IN HERE!")

Art lit himself a cigarette, in spite of the "No Smoking" sign tacked to the plywood front of the counter, and watched the smoke drift through the ceiling vent above his head, as lazy as the day. Even by Wonder Hut standards, things had been slow: in the morning, a stoned teenage couple who were ditching school; and shortly after noon, a family whose members were more interested in the restrooms than in his exhibits. Of course, that wasn't counting one of Aggie Simms's dogs, who'd pushed the screen door open with her bloodhound snout before the Hut's proprietor could shoo her away.

Art drew a deck of cards from under the wooden counter, shuffled them, and laid them out for a game of clock solitaire. He hadn't made much progress before little Benny Powlett strode in and began searching through the rack of supernaturally themed postcards.

"Looking for anything in particular there, Benny?"

"Yeah, I saw a real cool one the other day. It was like a real old picture of a ghost, he was dressed up like a Civil War guy. He was standing on his own grave or somethin'. Anyway, he didn't have any head. Like just his neck was sticking out of his coat." Benny flipped through the display a little more. "Here it is." Following another search, this one through his pants pocket, the boy spread out 79 cents on the counter.

Art scooped up the playing cards, then reached for the coins but stopped just short of touching them. "I tell you what, Benny. How about if we cut cards for it? Double or nothing?"

"No-oh sir," little Benny replied. "I don't have that much money. And my dad told me I should never cut cards with you for *anything*. He says you never lose." Pushing the heap of nickels and pennies toward Art, he asked, "Is that true?"

"That your dad told you never to cut cards with me? How would I know?"

"No, I mean you always win."

"Well," Barker smiled, "there's only one way to find out, isn't there?" He positioned the neat stack of cards face down in front of the boy.

"Uhn uh, thank you no, sir. I'll take my dad's word for it."

Art shrugged. "OK, if that's the way you want it." He rang up the 79 cents and distributed it among the register's coin trays. "Maybe next time, Benny, if you're feeling lucky."

The boy disappeared without saying goodbye.

Officially the Wonder Hut closed at five, but by three-thirty, Art was ready to cancel Lola's four o'clock show and lock the place up for the night. He'd just switched off the light above the chicken's dance palace when he heard the screen door open slowly. Covering Lola's cage with a moth-worn blanket, Art turned his head to see who'd arrived.

A slender man of medium height, dressed in a stylish dark gray suit, softly shut the door behind him. He looked as if he were ready for a business meeting, except that his jacket was unbuttoned and he wasn't wearing a tie. The stranger's face and hands, Art noticed, were significantly sunburned, as though he'd just spent an unaccustomed weekend in the outdoors; even the scalp showed red through his thinning black hair. Without comment, the man swivelled to his left and started walking down the line of exhibits at the front of the building.

Lola clucked quietly from beneath her blanket; Art cleared his throat. "Excuse me, sir. The tour is a dollar fifty." It wasn't really a tour, of course; the customers just wandered around on their own recognizance. Nonetheless, Art liked to call it that for professional reasons.

The city man paused in seeming confusion; eventually, though, he pulled out his wallet and handed over two dollars. Not waiting for his change, he headed off in the same direction as before, merely glancing at the meteorite, the sliced geode, and the other mineral-oriented display cases. He slowed, however, as he rounded the corner, passing the carnivorous plants, and came to a crawl when he reached the exhibits arrayed along the back. This was where Art kept the animal collection, mostly preserved specimens in large jars of formaldehyde. A bemused smile settled into the man's face as he approached the two-headed snake. For several minutes he studied the freak floating in its jar, then sauntered down the line.

The visitor had nearly completed his inspection when Art approached and handed him two quarters. "You forgot your change. By the way, it's getting close to three-thirty. Did you want to see Lola's show at four o'clock?"

"Lola? Oh, you mean the barnyard Terpsichore? No, no, thank you. I'm allergic to chickens, I'm afraid. I believe it's the feathers."

"Well, suit yourself." Art returned to his seat by the cash register. Meanwhile, Mr. Sunburn skirted the chicken's home with a hand held across his nose, and quickly swung by the last few jars of pickled beasts. But Art could have sworn the guy winked at the desiccated Gila monster before stepping up to the souvenir section.

Without thinking, Art fished a cigarette from his shirt pocket and stuck it between his lips. The match was almost struck when he remembered the sign. He slipped the cigarette back into the pack, and waited to see if he would make a sale.

The visitor moved methodically down the line of merchandise, skimming over the ashtrays and boxes of cheap gemstones, pausing for a quick flip through the postcards. Just as he seemed about to leave, he plucked, with a quiet chuckle, a key chain from a wicker basket right beside the register. A red plastic devil, grinning and clutching a menacing pitchfork, dangled from the metal ring. The sunburned man placed it on the countertop and extracted his wallet again.

"Two fifty," Art said. The stranger handed him a five. Before opening the cash drawer, Art added, "Unless you want to cut for it: double or nothing."

"Excuse me?"

Art laid down his deck at the plastic devil's feet. "You know, cut cards for it. If you win, it's free; if you lose, it's five dollars."

"Ahh…" The slender man smiled. "I believe I overheard something about you at the café next door. Something to the effect that you never lose."

Art smiled back noncommittally. "Ohhh, I don't know about *that*. I'm pretty lucky, I guess. But…"

"It sounded like a little more than luck to me, Mr. Barker. More like you were charmed somehow."

Art shrugged.

"Still," the stranger said, "I'm a bit of a gambling man. I accept your wager."

Extending his hand, palm upward, toward the cards, Art offered the man first choice. The stranger cut to the queen of diamonds; Art drew the king of spades.

"Fair enough," the man said.

Without a word or a sign, Art deposited the five in the till. He'd expected Mr. Sunburn to get a little angry, but instead the guy looked amused.

"I say, Mr. Barker, I don't suppose you'd like to try that again? Just for fun, of course; no bet."

Art nodded an OK. The thin man picked the two of diamonds this time; Art cut to the three of hearts. The stranger went again, drawing the ten of clubs. Art lifted the card from the very top of the pack. When he flipped it over, the king of diamonds glared at them with his one good eye.

"Once more," the well-dressed man requested. "You first, this time."

Art obliged, cutting to an ace; the stranger exposed a six.

"Well, I see your friends next door weren't exaggerating."

Wearing an "aw shucks" expression that was less than one-third honest, Art began to slip a rubber band around the cards. The stranger reached out to prevent him.

"I don't suppose you'd be willing to consider a *real* wager, would you?"

Art hesitated. "Like what?"

"Allow me first to present you with *my* card." The plain white rectangle was simple and to the point:

SATAN
CONSULTING & ACQUISITIONS

Art laughed, but not so loudly as to be considered totally rude—totally rude, that is, if the card were meant to be serious.

"So, I suppose it's my *soul* you want to play for, huh?"

"*Very* astute of you, Mr. Barker, very astute."

Was this guy just pulling his leg, or was this some kind of weird scam? Then again, maybe he was out-and-out nuts: the way he'd winked at the Gila monster ...

"Hmmm, well, I don't know." Art squinted warily at the man in the suit. "What do I get if *I* win?"

"Why, how about something to spice up your little gallery here? You could choose anything you like: a perfectly preserved baby dragon, perhaps, or maybe the mummified hand of Genghis Khan? All items guaranteed genuine. What do you say?"

Art's lips adopted a dubious twist.

"Oh, I'm not talking about mundane articles, Mr. Barker, not about all the money in the world, or anything tawdry like that. I mean something *special*, something that would really put the Wonder Hut on the map." The man picked up the key chain, twitching the ring so the little devil danced. "Although, I wouldn't balk at, say, a diamond twice the size of your head. After all, *that* would be quite an attraction, wouldn't it?"

Trying—half successfully—to suppress a smirk, Art asked, "OK, what's the joke?"

"No joke, Mr. Barker, no joke, I assure you. If you don't believe me, I have a contract right here all ready for your signature." The sunburned man extracted a folded piece of paper from his inside pocket. He handed the document to the Wonder Hut's owner.

When Art opened it, a faint odor of burning sulfur wafted through the air, familiar from his chemistry-set phase.

"You'll find it's mostly the usual sort of boilerplate, although I do want to call your attention to a few specifics. First, any benefit you may accrue will remain in your possession to use as you wish for the rest of your natural life, and may only be passed on to your direct heirs and/or assigns, who will have the same privilege of use, but not of bequest; in other words, nothing is granted in perpetuity. Second, no guarantee is made that said item will be appropriate for the uses you may intend for it; if things don't work out the way you had hoped, there are no returns, refunds, or exchanges.

"Finally: no immortality. I had a few requests for it in the early days, and the problems they entailed for everyone involved—myself included—forced me to disallow such arrangements."

Art turned his attention to the contract with a bemused smile, but grimaced and turned his own shade of red when he saw his middle name in twelve-point type: *Who the hell* … But putting that aside, after looking over the rest of the document, then looking over Mr. Sunburn, he found himself favoring the dedicated-lunatic hypothesis.

"You see, Mr. Barker, I've left ample space for you to describe any item you might care to choose. So tell me: what would satisfy your collector's ambition? What would make the Wonder Hut truly worthy of its name?"

Art asked himself why he'd never had a phone installed at the Hut, and had avoided buying a cell phone: either one would probably be coming in handy right about now.

"Well, I'll tell you, Mr. … "

"Satan," accompanied by a small nod.

"Well, I'll tell you, Mr. Satan, I just don't seem to be able to come up with anything right now that would be worth risking my soul for. How about you let me think about it for a few days?"

The stranger pursed his lips. "I must say, Mr. Barker, I took you to be rather more … decisive than that. But I'm nothing if not a reasonable man. Let's say you don't have to specify your treasure right now. If you win, you can mull it over until you decide on *exactly* the thing to make your little museum famous. Then you just fill in the blank, and it will appear upon the instant, right here in the Wonder Hut. How would that strike you?"

The Hut's proprietor scratched his head and winced. How was he going to get rid of this guy? "I don't…"

"Come, come, Arthur," Satan interrupted, placing a familiar hand on Barker's forearm. "You don't mind if I call you Arthur, do you?"

Art shrugged and shook his head.

"I ask you, Arthur, how can you pass up such an opportunity?"

All right, Art decided: he'd go through with the game just to get the crackpot out of the place. After all, what difference could it make? If he lost, let the guy believe the title to Art's soul had changed hands. And besides, he always won…

"OK, Mister… Satan. It's a deal."

"Excellent, excellent. Just place your signature on this line."

On the line above it, the name "Satan" had been written in unadorned cursive; the seal of the local county clerk appeared underneath.

"You, uhh…you don't expect me to sign in blood or anything, do you?"

"Oh no, no, Mr. Barker, of course not: that would be unsanitary, as well as a bit… dated." The man in the suit drew a cheap red pen from his shirt pocket. "Here, this will do quite nicely."

While Art was signing, the man in the suit produced another paper from his inside pocket and unfolded it. "Please sign this copy as well. The blank will automatically be filled in when you specify the 'item' of your choice."

Art affixed his signature to Satan's copy and handed it back, then folded his own four times and stuffed it in the pocket of his shirt. "Well, I suppose that's it, then. By the way, why seven rounds?"

"As the contract indicates, that way the first one to reach four is the winner; and four is my lucky number."

"Oh … OK." *Four… four… Four Horsemen …?* Art wondered, then bobbed his head a notch before saying, "So … why don't we just get started?"

"My feeling precisely. And now, why don't you shuffle the cards? And take the first cut, if you'd like?"

When he thought they were sufficiently randomized, Art set the cards on the counter and split the deck near the top. He came up with the ace of clubs, made certain Mr. Sunburn had seen it, then placed the thin stack back atop the remainder of the deck.

Take that, Mr. S.

The slender man's eyebrows bunched together, then he divided the deck close to the bottom. He turned his hand over to reveal the ace of diamonds. Art frowned.

"That wasn't a very auspicious start, was it, Mr. Barker?"

"Yeah, well … ties don't usually count."

"True enough, but we're being a bit more formal than usual, aren't we?" Satan smiled and patted the pocket containing the contract. "Bridge ranking—diamonds beat clubs. My shuffle, I believe." He divided the deck, and the cards flashed in an arc between his hands. The motion was repeated several times, so rapidly that Art wasn't sure exactly how many. All at once, as if by magic, the cards shot into a neat bundle on the counter top. *Crazy or not,* Art had to admit, *this guy's pretty damn good.*

"From now on, let's say dealer cuts last, all right?"

Art turned his hands palm-up and shrugged.

"Go ahead then, Mr. Barker, your turn."

Splitting the pack in the middle, Art found the four of hearts. After he'd replaced his cards and squared up the pile, the sunburned man quickly pulled the two of spades. The loser's frown suddenly morphed into a grin.

"That's one each. This is becoming quite an interesting contest, eh, Arthur?"

"Well, it's still pretty early." Art shuffled the cards and set them on the counter. He wished Mr. Sunburn were already out the door, yet he couldn't help being curious to see how the game would end. His opponent plucked the seven of clubs; Art came up with the ten of the same suit.

"Two to one in your favor, if memory serves. My shuffle again."

When Satan had finished and set down the cards, the two men cut once more. And once more Art drew the higher card.

"Bastard! You bastard!" Mr. Sunburn shouted and smacked his hand flat on the counter. Art couldn't help grinning in reply. But then the slender man spat out, "You're cheating! I don't know how, but you're cheating!"

Art stopped smiling. "Hey, don't call *me* a cheat, you son of a bitch con-artist, or whatever you are!"

The thin man cocked a delicate fist. Instinctively Art put up his guard, even though the guy looked as if *Lola* could kick his ass around town. The pair stood motionless for what seemed like minutes. Finally, Art's opponent lowered his hand.

"I apologize, Arthur. I don't know what came over me. Became a little too caught up in the whole thing, I suppose. And your luck isn't something I'm very accustomed to."

Art grunted.

"OK, so, let's see, it's three to two now, right?"

"Wrong: *I* have *three*; *you* have *one*."

A pause. "Oh yes, you're quite right. Sorry." Satan smiled, although his smile was as slender as himself. "Three to *one*." The man pulled a handkerchief from the breast pocket of his suit jacket and ran it over his thinning hair. "You're living up to your reputation, aren't you. But the game isn't over yet, is it." He replaced the handkerchief and said, "Go ahead, Mr. Barker: shuffle the cards."

Still vibrating with stifled anger, Art picked up the deck. He was just about to begin mixing them up again when the screen door opened. The quiet creak of the hinges caused the two men to turn. Benny Powlett was back.

"Hi there, Benny," Art called cheerfully, without feeling particularly cheerful. "What can I do for ya?"

"It's almost four o'clock."

"Yeah ...?"

"I came to watch Lola dance."

"Sorry, I already put her to bed for the night."

Little Benny looked exceedingly glum. "Gee, Mr. Barker, can't you wake her up? It's still early yet."

"I'm busy right now, Benny. Can you hold on a few minutes?" Art split the pack precisely in half, and let the cards slowly snap together, one edge atop another, making a single interleaved pile.

"But I have to go home for *supper* soon," Benny explained.

The cards fluttered together a second time, then a third. The boy swung his right leg back and forth, sneaker giving off an aggravating squeak each time it made contact with the floor.

"Hey Benny, cut that out, will ya?" The cards riffled again. From the corner of his eye Art could see the boy fidgeting silently now, which was even more annoying than the chirping shoe. He stopped mid-shuffle. "Look, I'll tell you what. Why

don't you take the blanket off Lola's cage and wake her up?"
As Benny happily trotted away, Art went on mingling the cards.

"Now what?" the boy called.

Ffflitt. "See that little lever there on the side? Pull that down so she can get out on the stage."

While the lever rattled quietly, Art laid down the deck and stood back to see what would happen. An ace for Satan, followed by a nine for himself: one more win for the enemy.

"Well, well," the man in the suit remarked. "*Now* it's three to two." After bowing ever so slightly, he added, "Still your favor, of course." Satan picked up the cards and began to mix them, this time imitating Barker's pedestrian style. He smiled condescendingly. "Getting nervous, Arthur?" nodding to himself, eyes locked on his opponent's face. At last he slapped the deck down. "Go ahead: cut."

This time Art plucked another ten, while Satan found himself a one-eyed jack. Without waiting for comment, the man nudged the deck toward Art with his fingertips. "All tied up again," he said, "and only one trick remaining."

For the first time, Art really looked into the man's eyes. There was a fire in them: not literally, of course, yet they burned with a disquieting intensity. *Is this guy gonna get violent if he loses? And what's he gonna do if he **wins**?* As he reached for the cards, a heavy drop of sweat trickled from his left armpit, all the way down to his waist.

"Just a moment, Mr. Barker. I have a suggestion. How about if we let young … Benny? … shuffle this time? Just to add a touch of drama to the proceedings?"

Art hesitated, then called over his shoulder, "Hey Benny, can you come here a minute?"

"It'll be four o'clock soon."

"This will just take a minute."

The boy complied, glancing at the clock on the wall behind the counter as he came.

Art turned to him. "Benny, you know how to shuffle cards, don't you?"

"Ohhh no, Mr. Barker, I'm not—"

"You don't have to play, Benny. Just shuffle the cards. We have an important bet going here."

"Well …"

"Come on. Then you can go watch Lola dance as long as you want."

Benny looked to the clock again before reaching for the cards. "I'm not very good at this."

"That's OK," Art said. "Just mix them together a bit. Take your time."

The boy split the deck and tried to do it the way he'd seen his parents do at home. He bent back the ends of the two stacks and let the cards snap down one or two at a time, slowly enough so that each individual *slap* could be heard. When he was done, he still had two separate piles. Embarrassed, he tried again, but only a few of the cards overlapped.

"I'm sorry Mr. Barker. I'm not too good at this."

"Well, you can just sort of, you know," Art demonstrated with his empty hands, "hold the cards loose and just shove them together."

Benny complied, dropping three or four cards to the floor in the process.

"Gee I'm sorry Mr. Barker …"

"That's all right, Benny, you're doing fine. Just do that a few more times."

The boy retrieved the fallen cards and did as he was told.

After six or seven shuffles, Art said, "That's good enough. Don't you agree, Mr. … S?"

Satan nodded with an amused smile. "Well done, young man. Now how about placing the cards back on the counter?"

Benny did so.

"Thanks, Benny," Art said. "You can go watch Lola now."

"Just another few seconds, young sir." Satan fished a nickel from his pocket. "Before you go, would you flip this coin in the air for us? You don't have to catch it." Benny took the nickel, and Satan held up a hand to stop him from tossing it upward. "Call it, Art? To see who cuts first?"

Without thinking, Art chose heads. Benny threw the coin in the air; it hit the edge of the counter and landed on the floor where everyone could see the result.

"Thank you, young man. Well, Mr. Barker, it seems you get to go first." As Benny returned to Lola's enclosure, Satan grinned at Art. "So, what do you think? Will this be the unkindest cut of all?"

Art reached out, touched the pack's blue-embroidered top with the tips of his fingers, then drew back. He considered the cards awhile, trying to figure out where one of those damned aces was hiding. Meanwhile, he avoided looking at the other man's eyes; he didn't want to see that fire again.

Ace of spades, ace of spades, ace of spades, where are you? Taking a deep breath, he cut the cards: four of spades.

"It's stuck, Mr. Barker."

Without taking his eyes from the cards, Art answered, "What?"

"The lever's stuck."

"Well … just put your weight behind it …"

The sunburned man snickered quietly as he gripped the

edges of the pile with his fingers. Lifting only the top few cards, he held them face down while he watched his victim squirm. Then his hand began to rotate, smooth and slow.

A metallic scrape—and an equally metallic *thunk*—came from the direction of Lola's abode. Benny squealed; Lola clucked; a crash was followed by a scratchy rendition of "Charleston" blaring from a CD player. Just as Art was twisting round to see what had happened, Lola tried to jump-fly onto the counter.

Barker grabbed at the flapping hen; the man in the suit stood petrified. Squawking all the while as if Art were wielding an axe, the flurry of white flew into Mr. Sunburn's face, bounced off, and hit the floor at a healthy trot. Benny and Art had to chase her down the length of the Wonder Hut, but in less than half a minute they had her cornered by the case labelled "Holocene flies."

Lola protested her unceremonious capture as Benny babbled an apology. "Gee Mr. Barker, I didn't mean ... I don't ... I mean ..."

"You must've pulled the wrong latch." Art returned the ruffled hen to her cage and tossed the blanket on top. "I think we'd better skip the show after all. She's all upset."

"OK," Benny agreed, shamefaced, but without hiding his reluctance. "But can I come see her tomorrow?"

"Sure, sure, that's fine. Now, why don't you run along home to supper?" As Benny slinked out the door, Art stepped back to the counter. Although the slender man still hadn't moved, his smile had resurfaced. His hand began to turn again. It hadn't gone more than a few degrees before his nose started twitching like a rabbit's. Art's shirt ruffled in the ensuing sneeze, and the bottom card fell back onto the stack. Apparently the stranger didn't notice; Art, unsure of what to do, said nothing.

The man extracted an expensive handkerchief from his inside pocket and wiped his writhing nose. "I apologize, Mr. Barker, I…I…" After sneezing into the square of silk two more times, and looking on the verge of going for a third, his face gradually relaxed. Composed at last, he tucked the handkerchief away. Another small spasm flitted across his face, but without effect. The grin returned, and he exposed the bottommost card in his hand. The two of hearts.

"Hah! Hah!! I won! *I won!!*" Art whooped, clapping Satan on the shoulder like an old high-school chum. "Hey, I guess this means I 'beat the devil,' huh? Like in that old Humphrey Bogart movie, huh? Hah!!"

"Yes, yes. How many times have I heard *that* one before?"

"Oh! Pardon me for not being more original." Art struggled to hide the smile that pulled at the corners of his mouth, but not very hard. "Hey, c'mon now, Mr. Satan, don't be a sore loser."

The man in the suit made an unpleasant face that gradually evolved into a rueful smirk. "You're right, of course. Well, Mr. Barker, regardless of what some people might think of me, I always pay my debts. Doing otherwise would be bad for business, in the long run." He cleared his throat and concluded, "So, whenever you decide what it is you want for the Wonder Hut, just fill in the blank, and it's yours."

Art started to speak, clamped his mouth shut. His lips maintained a serious line, in spite of the amused wrinkles forming at the corners of his eyes. Retrieving the contract from his shirt pocket, he caught that whiff of burning sulfur again. "So, anything I want, it says. Except immortality. Is that right?"

"Yes, Mr. Barker, that's precisely what our agreement stipulates."

"OK, I've got it. Can I borrow your pen?"

"Certainly." With an elegant gesture, the slender man offered his red plastic pen. Art hunched over the paper and began to write, using neat block letters so there would be no chance of a misreading. As soon as he'd finished, he blew on the page to dry the substitute blood. The sunburned man walked around behind him and leaned over his shoulder, to see what the Wonder Hut's proprietor had written. When Satan saw what was there, he flew into a rage.

Business at the Hut had been increasing steadily over the last few weeks. Not *that* much yet, really, but definitely enough for Art to notice the difference. If things continued the way they'd been going, he might soon have thirty or forty people coming through on a good day. The new exhibit, as promised, was putting the Wonder Hut most decidedly "on the map."

Lots of people called it a fake, of course, and for obvious reasons. What sane person of any reasonable intelligence would believe the thing was real? Still, even those who doubted its authenticity admitted that it was a pretty good effect, and wondered how a hick like Barker had managed to create it.

The Hut's new "wonder" occupied Lola's former niche. (She'd been transferred to Lindemann's farm, where she was presently employed laying eggs, and apparently couldn't have been happier.) The thing was housed in a five-gallon glass jar with a heavy glass lid that was tightly sealed with red wax. The container looked like the sort of thing doctors had used for storing medical specimens around the end of the nineteenth century. There wasn't any formaldehyde in it, though.

At that particular moment, an elderly couple was standing in front of the display with their grandchildren, who *oohed* and *aahed* appreciatively. From his seat behind the register, Art heard the old woman ask, "I don't know, Alex. Do you think it's really …?"

"Aww," Alex interrupted, and flapped a dismissive hand. "That's phonier than the two-headed snake." The foursome stayed a minute or two longer, then wandered over to peruse the Gila monster.

Gazing on his new attraction with pride, Art dug a cigarette from the pocket of his brand-new shirt, recalled his own prohibition against smoking, and returned it unlit to the pack. All the while, he watched the thick black mist that swirled restlessly inside the glass container. Here and there tiny flashes of golden light would appear, illuminating the murk from within; they flitted through it briefly, and disappeared again.

Directly beneath the jar sat a little hand-drawn sign, in red block letters on a black background, proclaiming to the credulous and the skeptical alike: The Devil's Soul.

Author's Comments:

An association sprang into my mind between the word "cut" as in "cutting cards" and the word "cut" as in Shakespeare's phrase, "the unkindest cut of all." (I never know where these things originate, and I don't really worry about it very much, although I wish they happened more often.) From this came the idea of a serious penalty connected with cutting cards, which in turn led to the notion of a high-stakes competition; as a matter of course, this brought the Devil into the picture. But then the thought of turning the tables on him occurred to me, and the rest flowed more or less freely from there. (Full disclosure: I did steal Lola from a Werner Herzog film, "Stroszek.")

A Life Denied
by John Hanford

The recurrent dreams, actually mere ephemeral wisps and glimpses of scenes, began early in Greg Siefert's life. Invariably these depicted Greg's mother as a young woman lovingly caring for a boy whose face was never fully revealed. Greg was an only child, but sensed the child from the dreams was not him. Although the visions were transitory, Greg remembered them vividly with a sense of warmth and contentment. The dreams gradually occurred less often and finally ceased as he proceeded through adolescence and into adulthood.

Greg Siefert stepped into the empty elevator, breathed a sigh of relief that Thursday was over, then pushed the ground floor button. With any luck his ride down eighteen stories would only involve a couple of stops. The car paused on ten to admit a lone male. Greg glanced up, then refocused on his cell phone screen. The stranger, who wore a business suit and tie, seemed vaguely familiar. Greg's face creased with a slight grin because his office norm recently became business casual. Out of the corner of his eye he saw the new rider stare at him for a bit longer than seemed normal. Because of the gawk, he looked up. The man immediately turned to face him, revealing a visage that was an exact duplicate of Greg's, including the nick on the neck from this morning's shave. Greg gasped. The elevator jerked to a stop, but the door did not open. An acrid electrical odor filled the space.

With both hands, the man pointed to his doppelganger face and smiled. "What do you think, Siefert? I think this is how I'll get Dinger."

Dinger was the nickname Greg had given his ten year-old son, Dylan. Only he and Dylan knew of its existence. Greg was shocked and confused. A prickly feeling needled his back.

"Who are you? How do you know my son? Never go near him."

The man smirked. "C'mon, Dylan, let's go. Mom's waiting for us." He glanced at Greg to ensure the implied threat was understood. The door opened. The man departed, saying over his shoulder, "See ya later, Siefert."

Once out of the elevator, the man headed down the hallway. Stunned, Greg froze momentarily but decided to follow him. Stepping out of the elevator, he was met with the sight of a long corridor devoid of any other soul. He realized this hallway contained no doors, led to no suites or offices—strange for this building. This struck him with fear. Instinctually, he ran back to the refuge of the elevator and was surprised to find its doors still open. He stepped aboard and pounded the button for the ground floor. Then he noticed the indicator light on the elevator panel was not lit up for any floor. As the doors slowly shut, Greg's eyes grew wide. When the car resumed its descent, a nauseating feeling grew in his gut, his heart raced, and a drop of sweat dribbled from his underarm down his side. He had to get to his boy.

Greg raced to his late model minivan. He used its voice activated phone feature to call his wife as he sped out of the parking lot.

"Is Dylan home?"

"No, silly. You know he's got practice this afternoon. And, Helen called me to fill in for her for a couple hours, so I won't be able to pick him up. I texted you; didn't you get that? I told Dylan you'd be there to get him. You okay? You sound crazy frazzled."

"Crap, crap, double crap. I didn't see your message. I'll head to the park now. Yeah. I'm fine. We'll talk later when you get home."

"Well you don't sound fine." He punctuated Judy's final words by disconnecting.

Greg increased his vehicle's speed, and abruptly altered course to get him to the park where the little league Amigos were practicing. The prickly feeling again attacked his back. He constantly checked his rear-view mirror as his speeding crossed the line into reckless driving. Through flared nostrils, Greg began breathing heavily. He skidded to a halt in the ballfield parking lot and began running to where the team was located. He scanned for his son. Finally, he identified Dylan in the dugout, simply a bench enclosed by cyclone fencing. Greg slowed to a walk and exhaled a large sigh of relief through pursed lips and bulging cheeks. His son had not noticed his arrival.

Greg thought it prudent to cool down, settle down, before he greeted Dylan. He strode over to the fence near first base to watch the infielders work on grounders. The fence was just over waist high. He stood there and glanced over at Dylan who was still in the dugout, now arranging bats in the rack. The late afternoon sun had lowered enough to offer some relief from the day's heat. As his gaze returned to the field, Greg noticed a figure in a suit on a small hillside that bordered the left field. This figure appeared to throw a ball to the infield's direction. Before Greg could react, the ball continued past the infield and struck him in the right pectoral, knocking him to the ground. The distance covered by the throw exceeded what could be thrown by anyone Greg had ever witnessed. While still on the ground in considerable pain, he looked at the figure, who raised a hand in acknowledgment. Next, he saw the man throw another baseball with preternatural velocity and a flat trajectory. This throw struck the dugout fence directly in front of Dylan's face, who flinched, being startled by the loud sound so near his head. Greg could see the impact left a deformation in the dugout fence. Anger now displaced the pain in his chest.

The man who threw the ball walked off the knoll. Greg impulsively sprang into a dead run to confront him. He ran past the dugout, down the third base line, and came to the end of the ballfield only to find no one there. He walked up onto the knoll to get a better view of the surrounding area. No one, nothing. He glanced back toward the field; Dylan was not there nor in the dugout. Greg's eyes moved to the expanse of grass behind the ballfield. Beyond this grassy area was the parking lot. Dylan was being led to the parking lot by the man in the suit. Greg screamed his son's name and began running toward him. Dylan did not acknowledge him. Greg frantically yelled again as he got closer. This time Dylan turned to indicate he heard his name. Greg continued running to his son.

Finally, as he got closer to Dylan, he breathlessly asked, "Where you going? Who's that guy you were walking with?"

"What guy, Dad? Why you been running around like a crazy person? Coach sent us out to pick up foul balls." It was the second time in the span of thirty minutes one of his family members attached the word "crazy" to him.

Greg then saw the other boys fetching balls and placing them into their gloves or caps. There was no other adult, no man in a suit, near Dylan.

"Uh, just thought I spotted someone I knew. No biggie." Greg smiled wanly at his boy.

Dylan continued with practice as Greg watched from the bleachers. For the first time since he lay on the ground, Greg again felt the pain where the ball struck him. He peeked into his shirt to see a reddened welt. He would ice it when they got home. His phone buzzed, indicating he was being texted. The message was from Judy. "You guys grab something to eat on your way home. I'll be later than I thought. Don't get me anything. They're feeding us here."

Practice eventually ended with the boys doing base-running drills.

Father and son drove to Taco Bell, Dylan's preferred outside-the-home food. Greg didn't need to ask the boy what he wanted; his order never varied. They used the drive through. Greg used plastic at the pay station, then proceeded to the pick-up window. A gentleman handed Greg a large bag of fast food and said, "Here ya go, Siefert. Enjoy. You too, Dinger." Greg recognized him as being the man in the suit from earlier in the day.

"You son-of-a-bitch. I'll come in there and wring your neck."

"Dad, what the heck? Why you being crazy weird?" Greg saw fear in his son's eyes.

"That's the guy I saw with you earlier when you were picking up foul balls."

"That's Kenny Ptascek's older brother, the one who's graduating this year. He sure wasn't at ball today."

Greg looked from Dylan to the food server, who appeared to be a slim high schooler scowling at him.

"Sorry, bud. I mistook you for someone else."

After dinner, with Dylan in his room doing homework, Judy sat next to Greg on the sofa; he was reading the opinion page of the *Wall Street Journal*. He thought this could be his chance to discuss the day's peculiar occurrences.

"So," Judy said, "Dylan tells me you were acting a little strange earlier. Anything going on?"

Greg saw that Judy was not only concerned but was also seeking accountability, her eyebrows raised and head tilted slightly back, the pose used when she required he level with her.

"I was gonna talk to you ... about a couple of things, out-of-the-ordinary things, that happened today."

Judy produced an empty pill bottle. Greg recognized it as the prescription for treating his bipolar condition. Judy opened the bottle and turned it upside down. Nothing fell out.

"This scrip has been out for at least a week. What the fucking fuck, Greg? You know the crap problems that pop up when you don't manage your meds. You promised this time would be different."

"I know I screwed up not getting that refilled. But look at this." Greg unbuttoned his shirt to show her the baseball welt, hoping this somehow would defuse her frustration at his carelessness with the meds.

He swiveled a bit toward his wife. "See this. Let me tell you how this got here."

"See what?" Judy's frustration boiled into anger.

Greg looked down to point out the welt. There was no redness or mark on his chest.

Before he left the house for work the next morning, at Judy's insistence and in her presence, Greg called in to get his prescription refilled.

"I'm not convinced a refill will do the trick," Judy said. "If you, or I for that matter, notice anything else unusual, I'm going to get you an appointment with Doctor Voschall. And, I think I'll come with. You have to be upfront with him … and me. I won't put up with another shit show. It would break Dylan's heart."

Judy's frustration was born out of repeated manic episodes over the first few years of their relationship. Greg finally got his condition regulated with the appropriate medication. He had gone through several shrinks and numerous meds before getting the right doc to prescribe the right med that kept him level. The bipolar situation had never become severe to the point where he ended up with hallucinations or delusional thinking. However, it was serious enough that his over-the-top behaviors strained the marriage almost to the breaking point.

"You're right." Greg knew he had messed up big time by letting his prescription lapse. However, he sensed that the events of the previous day had indeed occurred, not simply been the result of a couple of weeks of missed medication. He did not voice this opinion; he felt doing so would only make an uncomfortable situation even stickier. "I'll pick up the meds on my way to work."

After the pharmacy Greg drove to his office with a new refill in his pocket. He entertained the notion that perhaps the man in the suit was actually due to his carelessness with his meds. This was a less threatening thought than the alternative … that an exact-looking duplicate actually existed and attempted to get into his head and harm his loved ones. Once in his building, he hurried to catch an elevator; a young woman was on it. On the tenth floor, the woman exited. Greg looked up from his phone to catch a glimpse of her as she left. Staring back at him was the man in the suit.

"You don't think that refill will 'do the trick' do ya? No, brother, I'm not leaving until I'm finished. And by the way, I'm here to let you know that I'm not only getting Dylan, I'll get Judy, too. You won't like what I'll do to them, Siefert. I'm a nasty one. But it's really you I want to hurt. You deserve it for what you've meant to me." He arched his eyebrows.

Greg became enraged at the reappearance of this spectral copy of himself. Simultaneously, he smelled the burnt electrical odor and became paralyzed not just with fear but actually unable to move, even to breathe. The stranger reached over with his cold dead index finger and traced on Greg's shirt the circumference of the welt from the previous evening. The coldness of the digit sent a shiver. The man punctuated this movement by forcefully poking the middle of the circle, sending Greg into severe pain.

"Siefert, the minor inconvenience on your chest is nothing. Wait until Dylan and Judy really feel my glorious dalliances. I'm quite skilled at such matters. And, the best part, you'll have a ringside seat for it all. So long for now. I'll be back when it's time."

With this, the elevator abruptly stopped. The man got off, and the malodorous aroma vanished. Greg's paralysis left him as he gasped for breath and staggered against the elevator wall. The door closed and the elevator rose to Greg's floor. He went directly to the men's room to wash his face and regain his composure. As he looked in the mirror, he unbuttoned his shirt to inspect his chest. The welt, redder than the day before, now had a fingertip-sized purplish dot in its middle.

In addition to his bipolar medication, Greg was also prescribed something for anxiety when needed. He removed a Xanax from his wallet. He kept a couple of these with him when he felt a panic attack coming on. Greg was past the "coming on" stage. He walked to his cubicle without exchanging greetings with his officemates and simply closed his eyes to follow his breath while waiting for the anti-anxiety meds to take hold. He determined he would not share this most recent event with Judy, Dr. Voschall, or anyone else. His pectoral throbbed, but within a few minutes the pill kicked in. Greg checked his email to begin his day's work. He felt doing otherwise would fuel his anxiety.

Greg dutifully took his bipolar meds over the next month. During this period he had no more face-to-face run-ins with his lookalike. Occasionally he would catch a glimpse of the man, or at least Greg thought he did. The man was driving a bus past him in the opposite direction, casting the briefest look at him. A similar encounter happened while Greg was in line at the supermarket. He saw the man walking out of the store, this time arching his eyebrows as he fleetingly looked at Greg. However, even these events became fewer and eventually stopped. Greg had not felt the need to take any Xanax for ten days.

It was during these few weeks that he again began having the recurrent dreams from his childhood. As before, these scenes of domestic tranquility were pleasant for Greg. He enjoyed seeing his young mother, who passed away shortly after his twentieth birthday, caring for the little boy. The mother generously doled out loving attention to the child. Greg seemed to remember every detail of these dream fragments. The thought of them often brought a smile. Indeed, he pondered whether his adherence to the medication regime may have facilitated this additional smidgeon of contentment.

On a Friday evening, Dylan was out of town with the Amigos for a weekend tournament. Judy was working her shift at the hospital. Both she and Greg would join their son the following day. Greg looked forward to a little alone time. As he placed a bag of microwave popcorn into the appliance, he glanced at a weed eater battery that was sitting on the counter top being charged. At the exact moment his eyes fell upon the battery's small green LED, everything went black, totally black and silent. It seemed to Greg as if looking at the glow of the LED had caused the power failure. The air conditioner stopped; the pole light over their shed had also failed. The house was situated two miles outside the city limits, a quarter of a mile from the nearest neighbor. No light came in from outside the house.

Greg became momentarily disoriented to the point that he lost his balance and had to instinctively shuffle his feet to keep from falling over. In spite of being an adult, Greg still harbored a fear of the dark, especially when inside a building. Being indoors allowed the possibility for otherworldly beings to float near and silently slither about. His solitary situation now amplified the fear. A prickly feeling again needled his back. He reached into his pocket to retrieve his phone to use its light. It was not there. His heart raced; a bead of sweat slid onto his upper lip. Greg checked his other pocket. The phone was there.

"Settle down, doofas. It's just a fuse," he reprimanded himself.

In spite of his fear, he decided to go down into the basement to check the fuse box. He would be an adult in this situation, not a scared little boy. If the problem was not a fuse, he would retreat to the relative safety of the outdoors and phone in a power outage to the electric co-op. He would also call Judy. The fuse box was in the mechanical room of the basement. Greg headed down as quickly as he could before he chickened out. The phone light allowed him to see, but its peculiar illumination also cast unusual shadows throughout the interior terrain he had once known so well. Now the place was unfamiliar and strange to him. He opened the door to the room where the fuse panel was located, moved the phone light around to ensure no one was there, and walked over to check the main fuse.

The fuse was not blown. Suddenly, the sickening bitter electrical odor of the man in the suit assaulted his sense of smell. This sent Greg into full panic mode. He turned to escape but ran into the door; he hadn't shut it when he entered. Greg expected to be grabbed. He reached for the doorknob, threw the door open and ran up the stairs. In his haste, he dropped his phone; it now lay at the bottom of the stairs, its pointless light shining upward. He needed the phone, but he sensed going back down would further endanger him. In spite of the terror, Greg descended the stairs to retrieve it, being sure not to glance about once in the basement. The electrical stench grew overpowering as he bent to reach for his phone, and a buzzing sound filled his head. Greg grabbed the device, sprinted up the stairs, and ran from the house.

He continued until he reached a mature oak tree under which he and Judy had placed a decorative bench. There he noticed a hint of a breeze, and an orangish quarter crescent moon beginning to emerge from behind a cloud. Greg looked back at the house and then the surrounding area. Other than the total electrical failure, nothing seemed amiss. He relaxed a bit and sat down to call the co-op. The moon, now fully free from the cloud, cast out more light. His night vision became more adjusted to the dark, and he was able to see more than when he first had emerged from the house. Greg Googled the co-op's number and dialed it directly from the web page. He again looked up at the house: all clear. The call did not go through; there was only dead silence on the phone. He attempted to call the number again. Nothing.

Movement from the front door of the house caught his attention. The door slowly opened. The man in the suit walked through it. He looked in Greg's direction and walked toward him. Although Greg recognized who was approaching, he did not have the instinct to flee; rather, he felt no need to do anything but sit and wait for the other. It was as if his fear could not emerge at the time he most needed it. He was numb. When the man was about five feet from the bench, Greg's hand went slack and the phone dropped to the ground. A buzzing sound grew in his head. The breeze had ceased and the burnt stench returned. Greg's nostrils flared ever so slightly at the odor.

"You got to live a life. I was deprived of that. You'll now pay for the injustice you caused." This confused Greg; he had no idea to what the man referred. "It's time, Siefert. Now it's my turn to live. Breathe in my essence, breathe in me. Breathe deeply."

Greg complied and inhaled the acrid odor again and again. As he did, he felt any agency he possessed over his body, and his life, slipping away. He became woozy. He sensed he was being led into a chamber with a small window in the door. The door closed him in. He looked out the window and saw what he had just seen a few minutes earlier, but it was as if his surroundings were at great distance. His recurrent dream flared up. For the first time in his life he saw the face of the child. His mother wept. Greg knew this child was the man in the suit. The scene made no sense to him.

Peering out of his mind's cell window, Greg could see that his body had stood up and was walking back to his house. He was now merely along for the ride as the man in the suit controlled his incarnate being. The lights in the house came on and the air conditioner began its drone.

Soon, Judy returned home from her evening shift. She did not initially see him.

"Hey, Greg-o," she called out. "I'm home, and have I got some stories to tell you." She walked to her husband.

"Hello, dearest." Greg never used this term when addressing her. "You'll perhaps have a couple more interesting stories to tell in the morning."

"Oh, yeah. How come?" Judy leaned in to give him a kiss.

The man put his arms around her and cupped the back of her head in his hands. Greg never had held her in this manner. Judy searched his eyes. He could see she had become uneasy. She attempted to back away but couldn't move out of his grasp.

"Well, let's just say things are going to change." With that he released her and moved to the sink and took the bipolar prescription out of the cupboard.

"Greg won't be needing these any longer." He poured the pills into the sink and switched on the garbage disposal without turning on the water.

"Greg!"

"He's left the house," said the man as he sneered at the now visibly alarmed Judy.

He walked over to her purse, removed her phone and car keys and placed them into the still running disposal.

Judy ran to the door. The man beat her there and blocked the path.

"I'm feeling amorous. Let's just get down to business. I've waited ever so long to have you." The man leaned down closer to her face and arched his eyebrows.

Judy peered into his eyes for some clue of her husband. "Who are you?" she blurted.

"I'm not Greg-o." He looked past her and said, "Sit back and enjoy the show, Siefert." He smiled broadly upon seeing Judy's terror.

The reality of the predicament gripped the encaged Greg. The man in the suit had taken Judy and would soon harm his son. Trapped in his own body, Greg could only watch the unfolding horrification of his existence.

Author's Comments:

The beginning of this story came to me many years ago while I was living in San Francisco. The first elevator scene where Greg Siefert meets a duplicate was born out of boredom while I cleaned offices one evening. At that time there was a story in the news of a local boy who disappeared. Apparently this influenced my imagination. I conceived the notion of a duplicate individual approaching a parent to let her know she, the duplicate, would find the parent's child to kidnap him. As a lure, the duplicate would use her identical looks to easily convince the boy to go with her. This is every parent's worst nightmare as, indeed, was the story in the news at the time.

When I was recently invited to write a ghost story, I remembered this idea. My story can be read two different ways: 1) the doppelganger is a specter of some sort with bad intent, or 2) the main character is an individual descending into insanity. Horror is an element of both readings. The recurrent dreams add a bit of a backstory to the piece that can fit either interpretation. I've intentionally left certain questions unanswered so the reader can add their own perspective to aspects of the story.

The Fourth Floor
by R.M. Kinder

Usually Martha Flanahan came to her campus office about 9:00 p.m. the evening before a class. This Tuesday evening, though, due to an engaging documentary, she arrived shortly after 10. At the entrance to her department, a flyer on the bulletin board caught her attention. "Ghost Hunters Society: Residual Haunting" was the heading. She smiled at the thought, not from amusement, but a kind of pleasure. There was a Ghost Hunters Society on campus? Good! She might seek them out. She went on to her corner office, a little excited at the thought of ghosts.

It was mid-September and already she was revising the syllabus for the advanced literature students. She was assigned only one class this semester, having carried an overload last semester and now serving as graduate advisor. She emailed the new syllabus to the office secretary with a request for 25 copies, correlated and stapled, by 2:00 the next day. Finished, she swirled her chair to face the huge window. The late summer moon hung there, so frightening if she let it be—how she and all humans floated in a massive universe, with planets and stars, and black holes, and supernovas, and yet, so vastly important to themselves. She felt important, precious even, to someone, even if to no one in her present. She had a future. She turned

131

back to the desk and opened the anthology to the reading assignment for her advanced class.

She heard a knock, faintly, maybe not at her door but at another office. She waited. It came again.

"Yes. Who is it?"

"Thurston. You still working?"

The voice was really nice. "Yes," she said. "If you're the janitor, please skip this office when I'm here." No answer. "Did you hear me? Skip my office when I'm here." Again no answer which made her uneasy. She hadn't heard him walk away, but then she hadn't heard him until the knock. She believed he was from janitorial services, but she didn't *feel* he was—because of that voice. Slightly chewing her inner cheek, she watched the doorknob, expecting it to turn if she stopped watching it. When she had waited quite long enough, she gathered her purse and phone, and turned off the desk lamp. She opened the door.

She smelled flowers. Honeysuckle. And the hall light was out.

She stepped back into her office and switched on the overhead light. It, too, didn't work, but moonglow from her office window allowed her to stride briskly to the hallway turn and to the department's main double doors. Glass windows bordered the doors, and the hall beyond shone faintly. The doors were locked, though. She rattled them. Thurston? She rattled them again and they opened. Not locked at all. She went out, let them swing back together, then tested with a pull. They did stick a little.

A few feet from her right was the faculty lounge, the interior murky but visible because of large windows on both the hall side and the outer wall, the latter giving in daytime to the sweep of lawn and walkways below. Someone sat at the farthest round table, head down and face obscured. Bulky, possibly very tall. He scooted the chair as if to stand, and Martha backed up a few steps. A flyer on the bulletin board near her fluttered. She wondered at that and the sudden draft. The halls were usually hot at night, air conditioning off or nearly so, and the heat rising from below stilling everything. She hurried down the flights of concrete steps, all lighted. She knew he hadn't followed her because the high ceiling captured every rustle, even on concrete steps.

Outside, she saw a small group of students near the chapel and another group just across the broad walkway. She waved at the latter as she passed them, turning toward the parking lot. They didn't respond, which was a bit disappointing. She was friendly with students and wanted them to like her. A campus was like a small town, the community almost a family. Her family, since she had none other. It was comforting to know that someone strolled on this lovely campus any given moment. Comforting.

When Martha picked up her photocopies the next afternoon, the secretary was busy typing hundreds of words a minute on a computer, a skill Martha had, too, but didn't have to earn her living by anymore.

"Is our janitor named Thurston?" Martha asked.

"It depends. They take turns on shifts. Fourth floor is a favorite because of the lounge."

"What's that mean?"

"Hot water, microwave, sofa."

"You mean they take breaks here? Don't they have their own lounge?"

"You bet. But ours is best."

"Is one of the men named Thurston?"

"Oh. I don't know that. I think our guy's Norm something."

So the fellow had been having maybe a cup of coffee and turned off the main lights to imply he was gone. Martha went into the lounge, to the rear table. Bare, no cup rings, no smudges. The far chair, though, was back from the table. Of course, anyone could have sat there today.

Outside the lounge, she stopped to read the flyer that had fluttered. One tiny straight pin through a corner held it to the cork, looser than the others. She pressed the bottom edge down to read.

Ghost Hunter Society: Residual Haunting
This is the week!
Monday through Friday, 11 p.m.
Outside Founder Hall

FOLLOW THE RULES:
SIXTY FEET OR MORE FROM THE ENTRANCE,
NO TALKING, NO NOISE OF ANY KIND, NO LIGHTS.

Ah. That would account for the students gathering last night. She found her office door locked as it should be. The blinds were still up as she had left them, but the small trash basket had been emptied of all but a light bulb. It had that indistinct inner darkness that meant it had burned out. Martha leaned over to look inside the lampshade on her desk. He had replaced the bulb? She opened the last, and smallest, drawer on the left side of her desk, where she kept personal supplies.

She couldn't remember how many bulbs had been left in the package. She opened every drawer and then scanned her bookshelves. All her stuff, odds and ends, useless but personal, seemed to be where it had been. And yet! Something was off. She wondered if Thurston had made small changes that she would sense but not be able to pinpoint. People did things like that—stealing one earring or slipping a tiny bit of something into a stew. Making their presence known but not to the seeing eye.

With no class scheduled the next day, Martha had no reason to visit campus that evening, but she couldn't resist. She sat on a bench near the Founder building. She could see the east corner window of her office and she glanced there often. Then, anxious from waiting, she had to see if that janitor, Thurston, was on the floor at all or had been there.

Inside the entrance a jean-clad girl thunked the drink machine with the heel of her hand and a rewarding clatter down announced the soda can. She smiled. "Hey Dr. Martha." The girl was from the advanced class, sat in the right rear corner. Sally. "Hey yourself, Sally," Martha said.

At each floor, Martha glanced down the hall to see if anyone was around. On the third floor, a far classroom door was open and whistling came nice and clear. Whistling was always good. She proceeded lightly, though the stair tread was deep, made that way over a hundred years ago when the outer building was constructed of quarry stones. Her steps echoed, she noted, especially the last half-flight to the fourth floor, maybe because the ceiling there was the highest. From the top, she scanned first to her left, where all classrooms appeared closed, dark, and then slowly across the lounge windows, the interior beyond empty. She went through the double doors into the office hall, turned on the switch for that hallway, and headed to her office, key in hand.

Her door was unlocked. The lamp was on, though she hadn't seen any gleam when she was outside, and she should have. Maybe Thurston had seen her and kept the office dark until she was ascending. Her desk phone, vertical in its base, was to the left rear, and her lecture notes squared before it. Her textbook centered at the front, and opened not to the work she was teaching, *The Turn of the Screw*, but to "The Beast in the Jungle." Janitors were supposed not to clean desktops unless asked to do so and certainly not to fool with textbooks and notes. The door was ajar, a sliver of hall exposed. She wondered if Thurston lurked just out of sight, waiting for her response. She gently eased the door closed, the soft click surely audible to him. She didn't lock it, though. He would know that, too. He was toying with her. It was a bit of fun, really. She sat down, a little breathless, slid the chair a few inches backward and half toward the window.

Rapatap.

She jumped, put hand to throat.

"Miss? You there?"

A different voice entirely. Reedy. She managed "Yes," then, "Who is it?"

"Walter Bryant, Miss. I hear you been asking after me. I'm your janitor."

After a second, biting her inner cheek, she rose and opened the door. He was blue-eyed and fair, small and grungy. Truly. The blonde hair, too long, was greasy. "I thought our guy was Thurston."

"No. It's always me or John Greer. We switch off."

"I really don't want anyone arranging my desk items or

poking around."

"I don't touch the desktop or the shelves or drawers, Miss. Neither does John but he hasn't been up here this week. It's my floor this week. I empty the trash."

"You didn't change the lightbulb? Move my books around?"

Head shake. "No Miss. It could be the secretary. She has ways, I've heard."

There was a closeness in his eyes that she didn't like. It was too personal and kind of knowing, though nothing could he know about her.

"I'll speak to her," Martha said. "You and Mr. Greer be advised that I prefer nothing be touched except the trashcan and the floor. And never interrupt me when I'm here."

"Yes, Miss!" He bobbed his head as he stepped back. "I only did tonight because you been asking after me."

"Thank you."

"You bet." His eyes swept down her and back up as she closed the door. She heard him walk away.

There was a small chance the bulb had been in the basket for weeks and had fallen back when he emptied the papers. She couldn't be sure.

At the east window, she peered down at the walkway. A young couple strolled below. They were obviously fond of each other, holding hands, too! That was so rare. Martha loved the sight of them and wished them well, a long and happy future. She hadn't met anyone yet who had the gentle openness she longed for, that perhaps existed only in literature.

Martha took a photo of her office, angling the shot to capture desktop and bookcases. She wouldn't have to trust her memory to know of any change. Then she turned the lock and left. The hall lights were on, the double doors opened easily.

The inner lounge was faintly outlined by moonlight through its windows. She felt bold. She opened that door.

A man stood up. "You need something?"

"No," she blurted and turned quickly, skimming the steps down as much as was possible. Who was that? She half expected to see him below or right behind her. The tiled foyer was so welcome, as was the night air, cooler now. Students were by the chapel again, and others near the bench across the walk. Martha said, "Good evening," as she passed the latter. They didn't respond. She wondered if she knew any of them.

Martha considered complaining about the misuse of the lounge, but decided her experience said more about her than about Walter and his cohorts. She was being a Miss-High-and-Mighty. Walter was only a poor guy making do with a terrible job. What she *could* do was see if her requests were absolutely honored. If so, she didn't need to be face-to-face with him again. She could delicately ask about him in a week or so, and not have it related to their having met tonight. Still, something strange was going on in her office and she wanted to know who was involved. She didn't want it to be Walter. Maybe a ghost.

Martha watched a late movie, an old black and white about an unseen visitor. She had seen it a few times before, and knew the plot, the actors' names, and many of the lines. She kept the sound off, since sound is what really frightens one, the music building—or the sudden silence which says *now, in a second, in a second.* But watching with no sound except the whispers of her own house, her own breathing, and knowing the story in advance, she was calm—nothing could shock her. She did believe in ghosts, but wasn't certain about their nature, except that they couldn't hurt anyone. They could frighten and surprise and warn, but not harm. She expected to hear a rap on her door here at home. From Walter or Thurston. The one *rapatap* had readied her for more. Even when she was under the soft cover of her bed, the room swimming in shades of gray, she waited for a knock from somewhere. *Silly woman*, she thought. *Stop trying to scare yourself.* She wondered what if one of them was a ghost? Thurston or Walter? Or if Walter and Thurston were one and the same?

The next afternoon, Friday, Martha led the discussion on *The Turn of the Screw*. As always, the students differed in their readings. Some believed the governess was simply disturbed, misinterpreting everything, hallucinating, even lying. "She wanted that uncle to pay attention to her." "She wanted to be special." Others believed the governess. "She's seeing ghosts, all right. And that kid is possessed. That extreme sexuality is a sign of the devil." The blonde in the corner, Sally, spoke. "I'll tell you who's guilty here. The uncle. He shifted the responsibility for his niece and nephew onto an inexperienced and passionate young woman. He took off to enjoy the world." She looked to Martha, and Martha gestured a quick, silent applaud. She enjoyed their fervor. She never mentioned the sheer balance of that novel until students had exhausted expressing their own beliefs and the textual evidence they offered as support. "Good work, guys and gals, as always."

Martha never worked on campus Friday, but waited until Sunday. This night, though, she wanted to go, to see if someone had again crossed boundaries. If it was Walter, she wouldn't complain about him to authorities, but she'd call him up for his behavior. She didn't want to cause more struggle for people who didn't have much and never would. But! She had earned a little respect. And maybe it wasn't Walter.

Dressed casually in slacks and tee shirt, keys and phone in her hip pocket, she walked to campus instead of driving. The night was so absolutely beautiful. The moon had a rare reddishness, possibly something that was a seasonal regularity and even had a scientific name. Walking beneath it seemed beautifully slow, and the slight breeze was melodic. Martha could hear music coming from nowhere and everywhere.

The campus union had just closed its doors and some young people carried a paper cup or a sandwich bag. Martha knew the paraphernalia they carried would soon litter the pretty campus. She liked it clean, fragrant, domed under a night sky. A young fellow came from the opposite direction, sat on the fountain circlet, as if he waited for someone. He wore a white shirt, open collar, dark slacks. His black hair was curly and a bit long, just below the ears. There was an old-world air about him. Martha liked him. He seemed both lonely and very attractive. Familiar, too. She was lonely herself, but not unhappy. She heard laughs and bits of words. An older woman walked her dog nearby and the dog stopped twice to tauten body and leash toward the fountain man. Martha studied him again. Was he the man who strolled hand-in-hand with his sweetheart last night? Now he faced her. She was certain he wasn't looking past her, but directly at her. If he tipped his head or lifted his hand as recognition of momentary contact, she would respond. He didn't. He just held the connection. Martha broke away, bowed her head briefly. When she raised up, something seemed to be between them, so she blinked, but still saw he was heading toward that end of Founder Hall, possibly to the entrance just around the corner.

The walkways had quietened, though a few more students

appeared just as Martha was about to enter the building. One group was settling down by the chapel, as they had the other evening, and another group by the bench across the west walkway. They had to be the Ghost Hunter Society, sixty feet away at least. Why two groups? To see angles. Of course. She studied both, saw Sally in one. Maybe something really was up and she'd see it, too. She wouldn't mind. They couldn't hurt anyone. Ghosts couldn't.

She went inside, her flat sandals whispering on the tile, and on up the stairs. She never took the elevator. It was notorious for stalling. She had done this many times, and yet, the stairs seemed different, and the halls. Could buildings be slow? The lights were on but not as glaring, softer? As if the glow came from the walls and not the ceiling. Was she later than usual, and some dimness was timed for the late hours? It was a more comfortable visibility. At the rise of the fourth floor steps, she was facing the lounge, the inside faintly outlined as usual. She wasn't going to look closer. The bulletin board was gone. It had hung there as long as she had worked here. She glanced down the hall to her left. Silent, a thin gray, and the floor seemed reddish. Even by her feet, the floor seemed buffed, like wax on cement. Had they painted it? Cement floors and even flagstones could be charming if painted. Had she read that or seen it?

The double doors to her department were closed, but not locked. She hurried on to her corner. The door had only a knob, no keyhole. Her hand trembled a little as she opened the door, slipped inside, leaning against the door to close it. The moonlit night pressed against her windows but the light was filigreed. Lacy shadows filled the interior of her office, lay on the floor. She glanced around. Nothing was really changed but she could see glimpses of things that weren't there, as if they emerged when she looked away. Two wood bookcases replaced three metal ones, the shelves deeper and the books fewer, larger. Yellow honeysuckle spilled out of a tall vase onto her desktop. The chair was oak, golden grain, curved, slatted back. The lampshade fringed with glass beads. Martha's vision blurred, she felt dizzy. She crossed through shadows to the window. A heavy tree filtered the moonlight and blocked the view of the south walkway. There should be no tree outside her office. She stumbled to her desk, sat down. Her clothing felt looser, softer. She held her breath for seconds, then breathed deeply, and pulled the anthology to her, opened it, brushed her fingertips over the delicate paper. Nostalgia flowed through her. She hugged the book to her breast. She was so full of wanting.

She needed to leave, though she didn't know why. She listened intently. No sounds. She rose, felt her heart flutter. She could call for help if she had to. She fumbled her phone from her pocket, held it in her left hand. She opened the door, stepped into the hall, not totally dark, the moonlight streaming over her from behind. No one. She crept to the corner, saw the wide open double doors, and hurried to and through them, turning toward the stairs.

He burst out of the lounge, tall and ragged, dressed in loose, bulky clothes, a cloud of motion. She tried to run, to skip-slide down steps as she had as a child, but she wasn't fast enough. He was behind her, past her, a rustle like leaves. Not Walter. The hugeness of him knocked her against the wall, scraping shoulder and temple. She fell backwards instead of headlong down, but scrambled up, to the railing. She saw him below and further down someone else fleeing, a slight woman dressed in blue, hair tumbling. Martha ran after them. She couldn't make her body move fast enough. She saw him catch the woman at the foyer, drag her outside. Martha reached the door, pushed and pushed and leaned her whole weight against it, staggered outside. She heard a woman's high voice, cries, a scream. Trees lined the walk in both directions. She couldn't see where they were. "Don't!" Martha yelled. "Don't! Help! Leave her alone! Get away from her." She struggled to move under the trees and couldn't. She couldn't hear her own screams, but could only feel the shaping of the words. "Don't! Don't! Get away from her. Leave her alone!" "Help!" Martha cried. "Help!"

The trees faded, as if moonlight bleached them. Martha was on the bare sidewalk. Her legs were weak, her mouth dry. A fine tremor ran through her like a current from the earth. She bent down, hands on her knees. The foyer light coned out a few yards away. No trees. No man. She tasted blood. She had bitten her lip. She ached throughout, as if her body had taken one mighty blow, had lost its life and regained it. She straightened, took a few steps, then a couple more. Someone came running toward her.

"Did you see them?" the girl blurted, her pixie face so alive, her eyes bright. "You did. I can tell."

Martha couldn't answer. There was the walk, the building, this girl before her, students beyond. The chapel.

"Dr. Martha?"

Martha focused on Sally, a student she liked.

"You saw something, didn't you?" Sally said. "Can we help you get home? You must have been right in the middle of it. We didn't see anything but you. You were yelling your head off. It was really scary. Can we get you something?" She looked toward the chapel, raised her arm as if to wave her friends over.

"I don't want help," Martha said. "Let me go on by myself. That's what I want to do."

"Could you talk to us first, just for a few minutes?"

Martha shook her head.

"Could we follow you home to make sure you're okay?"

"I'd rather you left me alone."

"Okay." She bent forward and whispered, "You're not really hurt, you know," and strode quickly away.

Martha thought she might not get off the campus at all. She might be sealed in a nightmare world. Creatures were swarming the night. That vile creature. Students. A young woman, wounded, mortally. Shadows loomed, floated. She didn't trust her eyes or her ears. She concentrated on her feet and the present movement in time. Walking home. Walking home is Martha. Martha walks home alone.

At her home, she sat in a chair in her living room, an afghan over her, every lamp on, and the television muted. She stared straight ahead, still expecting some attack, still hearing screams. When she was aware of morning, she was so sleepy and achy. She stared at the memory and tried to retain it all. She understood what had happened. It was absolutely clear. Her own curiosity and arrogance had brought her down. She had stepped into the week of it—the true record of the murder. Tuesday night someone had knocked on her door and she had answered. They had not responded but she had pursued. Thurston. She had opened the world.

Late Sunday afternoon she didn't go to the campus as she had once done on Sundays. In her home study, she searched online for records of a rape at the small university in Mason, Missouri. She found four, but one she recognized immediately, though the photos were black and white. Three people were involved: Leon Thompson, Lily Ferguson, and Thurston McKinney. Murderer, victim, fiancé. Lily Ferguson had been a student and teacher assistant. She had finished her tidying up of the office and was leaving when she was accosted by the groundskeeper, Leon Thompson, who raped and murdered her. Her fiancé usually came upstairs for her, but that Friday night he had paused longer outside, and had gone into the building from the west entrance. A few students heard Miss Ferguson's screams and cries but arrived too late to save her. They could identify Thompson, whom they saw fleeing the scene. Mr. McKinney had no word for the reporter, which is understandable. The campus president vowed to have the many trees shading the campus walkways removed.

Martha read the various accounts, studied the photos—the same ones except for a small one of Thurston and Lily in a canoe on Pilton Springs. Martha wanted to make copies of those photos and keep them. She decided that was not the right thing to do. Nor safe.

On Monday, walking from her car to the Founder entrance, Martha knew of huge trees shadowing the walks, of audiences here and there watching every move, comparing. Hungry to know. She remembered the man who had sat on the fountain, had met her eyes. Thurston. Who had first knocked on her door. It was not possible that she had caused him to leave the fountain and take the other entrance. She was now, not then. But he remained, is here. And that other one? The monster—somewhere in this town and time. What else might she encounter at any moment, if she didn't take care to close herself in. She entered the building, went up the stairs, remembered the slender girl in yellow. Was she in the building? At the fourth floor, Martha saw the bulletin board again. The flyer was gone. Someone came from the lounge with a cup of coffee, nodded at her. "Hey Martha." The chair of the department. Maybe.

Martha went in the main office. Her phone lay inside her mail cubby. She turned to the secretary. "Did you put my phone here?"

"No."

Martha took it out carefully. "Did you see who did?"

"No. Where did you lose it?"

"I'm not sure."

Her blinds were up, the anthology open on her desk. She turned on her computer, found the Campus Activities link and read the entries. No Ghost Hunter Society listed.

In the advanced class, she said "Quiz," and someone groaned. Someone else said "Good." They took out paper and pencil, waited for the question. She wrote it on the board which she often did, liking the old chalk on the black surface, the small clicks as the chalk was lifted and set again, the smoothness of her script despite the tremor she still felt.

Take a stance that James' Turn of the Screw is either fantasy or realism. Then explain briefly why it is important to you that the opposing stance not be true.

The corner chair where Sally sat was empty. Martha was sorry. She couldn't explain. She wanted to tell Sally and all the other students how to be careful, how to hold the world in the right frame. She thought she had known how.

While the students wrote, she stood at the window looking down where she had been last night, where a young girl had been raped and murdered. She saw the faint lines and movement of leaves and branches, heard short cries. Near the chapel something swept the grass, and a few shadows flitted where no one walked. They were all there, and perhaps throughout the buildings, on benches, gathering, remembering, finding one another and sometimes reaching out. Over the whole world? When she turned back to her students, some of them were watching her, and she shivered.

After class, standing outside the building, she rubbed the cold surface of her phone, turned it on. She touched the photo icon and selected the one new image. Her office, not as it was now, but as it had been, dark wood shelves, books, honeysuckle, porcelain dolls, a lovely young woman sitting at the desk and looking up at someone.

Author's Comments:

This story was inspired two things: types of hauntings and the balance between realism and fantasy in Henry James' *Turn of the Screw*. In a Residual Haunting, a traumatic event is recorded into the place of its occurrence and continues to replay without interaction with people in current time. In an Intelligent/Interactive Haunting, there is interaction. The haunting Martha encounters is a combination. At least one ghost interacts with her, perhaps accidentally. The combination raises questions of the nature of time, multiple planes of existence, and the transmission of thought. In fiction, as in real life, we must ask the classic question: is the narrator reliable?

Seeing Is Believing
by Chanda K. Zimmerman

She arrived precisely on time—not late, not early—and sailed into my office as if she were the Queen of England, past Kathy, my long-time receptionist who held the door open. Kathy gave me a wink and a barely concealed smile as she quietly shut the door.

"Mrs. Hillman, welcome. Please have a—" I paused because she had already plopped into one of the two chairs in front of my desk—the closest one. She was wearing a tailored suit in a kind of green tweed, something I'd expect to see in an old movie, with a rather rakish, old-style of fedora hat, and tight, delicate leather gloves in brown. Her shoes were leather, expensive and sturdy. Her hair was grey, not white, her glasses large and strong. She settled back to survey me with a frown creasing her weathered face.

"So, you're, Dr. Blacker, eh? You don't look old enough to be a doctor."

I smiled amiably, since I dealt with this all the time. It was not a blessing to have a baby face when you're in psychiatry. Even my attempt to add a Freudian mustache didn't help much.

"Well, Mrs. Hillman, what can I do for you? You told my secretary that you needed to speak to me about some …" I checked my notes, "some distressing hallucinations you're

149

having."

"Yes. Exactly. I want you to give me something to get rid of them."

"I'd be happy to help you. Why don't you tell me about them, and perhaps I can get an idea of what might be prompting this situation."

"I just want some pills, I don't want any of that 'talk therapy' or whatever they call it today. I know what's causing them—my husband."

"Ah," I started to say, but she wasn't to be detoured.

"He drove me crazy when he was alive and he's driving me crazy now that he's dead, and I want it to stop. I just need something to get rid of this nonsense."

"How long ago did he pass," I said gently, getting ready to reach for the box of tissues in my drawer.

"Six months ago. I thought the old goat would never kick the bucket." She looked at her watch, humphed, and gripped her black purse tightly in an effort to control her natural impatience with young whippersnappers like me.

The thought of a Black Widow flitted through my mind out of nowhere. But my professionally sharpened instincts— plus Mrs. Hillman's steely, gunfighter stare and grip on that purse—suggested she wasn't your classic "seduce and poison" type. No, more likely she'd use a shotgun in the driveway, then tie the body to the back fender and haul it and herself down to the local police station in broad daylight. I did wonder for a moment if there was an APB out on her right now. But I went for the more obvious question.

"Was he ill?"

"Well, of course he was ill! You don't die from being perfectly healthy unless you're dumb enough to do something totally stupid."

"I take it that Mr. Hillman was not a stupid man …"

"I didn't say that," she snapped. "I said he was ill. As for stupid, well…he wouldn't do all the things that last doctor ordered, said it would inconvenience me—as if dying wasn't an inconvenience!"

Now, we were getting to it. "So, he didn't seek treatment and you feel…," I searched for the right word for Mrs. Hillman's distinctive personality, "frustrated by that?"

"Frustrated isn't the word. The damn fool!"

Grief is an odd thing and often takes the form of anger at the other for leaving us. I felt confident now, except for Mrs. Hillman watching me expectantly, sort of like a stork hunting frogs in a still pond. I also felt a sudden chill like a strong breeze pass over me. I shook it off. Too many late nights, not enough sleep.

"Excuse me a moment." I rose, went to close the window that Kathy had opened this morning due to the beautiful weather, and noted absently that it was really warming up outside. Maybe I'd get a sandwich for lunch and have it in the park, good place to unwind after this session …

"So?" Mrs. Hillman demanded. Her beady little almost-black eyes indicated that this was a test. I sighed inwardly and put on my professional face.

"So, tell me about these hallucinations you're having."

She shrugged and actually looked slightly embarrassed. "The usual. Things out of place, not where I left them. Him sitting in a chair in front of the TV. Sometimes sitting in the car in the passenger seat. His voice, mumbling in my ear when I'm trying to sleep…thinking I see him in a crowded place, standing behind someone I'm talking to and waving at me in that simpering way he had. And no, I am not suffering from dementia. I had myself checked out. Nothing wrong with *my* mind." Her look implied she had doubts about mine. Of course, it wasn't uncommon to meet patients who felt that way.

"Do you see him or hear him now?"

"No! I refuse to give in to this nonsense. It's just figments of my imagination. I have decided to ignore it and if it starts, I just close my eyes and count to ten."

"And has that worked for you?"

"Most of the time. But it gets worse at night. Keep hearing that damn fool whispering to me, the same silly stuff he was nattering on about when they took him in the ambulance."

She closed her eyes and set her jaw as if trying to block him out now—or perhaps trying to find the inner reserves to cope with an annoyingly dense medical professional. "I just want you to prescribe something to make it stop so I can get a decent night's sleep. My doctor said he couldn't give me the stuff one of my friends got until I'd had a meeting with you."

She opened her eyes and stared at me, a challenge.

"Dr. Ernst?" I said, checking my notes again, and noting that the drug she was after was a rather powerful sedative. "I think that was a wise suggestion on his part."

"Wasn't a suggestion. The damn fool told me he wouldn't do it any other way."

I was curious. "Why was it prescribed for your friend?"

"Same problem!"

"Her husband died recently?"

"Two years ago—she was practically a basket case from lack of sleep."

"Her dead husband was speaking to her at night?"

Mrs. Hillman's beady stare bored into my eyes like a laser.

"No, she made the mistake of buying red slippers and found she couldn't stop dancing all night." At my blank stare, she rolled her eyes and sighed dramatically. "A literary reference. It's clear American education has simply gone down the toilet since I taught junior high. Good grief, man, of course from hallucinations! Why do you think I'm here? I do not wish to end up like her. So, will you help me or not?"

"Well, of course I'll help you but first …" I paused, staring at the *étagère* on the wall across from my desk, behind Mrs. Hillman. The small brass rooster on the middle shelf was… floating a few inches above the shelf. It twisted around, and upended itself, as if someone were looking at the bottom for a maker's mark—or a price tag. Then it settled back to the shelf. I blinked. Twice. And took a deep breath. Mrs. Hillman was a powerful influence, clearly.

"WELL?" said Mrs. Hillman, her eyes narrowing as if she suspected me of drinking my breakfast.

My focus snapped back to her. But from the corner of my eye, I saw a blur upon the air between my desk and the small therapy couch over in the corner near my bookshelves. I couldn't help myself. I glanced at the couch, sensing more than seeing a movement in the fabric, like someone sitting…no, *lying* on it. My heart skipped a beat. I focused deliberately on Mrs. Hillman's pinched and angry face.

"WELL? What's wrong with you? You having a stroke or something?"

I wondered. But suddenly a memory of one of my favorite professors came to mind. *"Anything that is real in its consequences, is real. Doesn't matter if it isn't 'real' in the normal sense of the word. It's very real to the person experiencing it."*

Suggesting the obvious couldn't be any worse than just

giving this woman a sedative that could easily be used to knock her out, or even to commit suicide. Ethically, I had to pursue the source of her problem, and hopefully come to terms with whatever she was doing to my own state of mind.

"Mrs. Hillman, do you…do you happen to believe in ghosts?"

She jerked back in her chair. "What? What are you, some kind of a quack? Of course not!"

"Well," I tried to present the idea more gently, "many people do believe in ghosts and when we believe in something, it often manifests itself in our life in many different ways."

Her eyes had become round, like an owl's. I took it from that look that she was waiting for my delusions to reveal themselves fully so she could report me to the proper authorities. But thinking of my old mentor gave me confidence. I plowed ahead in the hopes of making connection with her on either a rational or emotional level.

"That doesn't necessarily mean that there ARE ghosts. It just means we are experiencing something that our mind doesn't have a way of understanding or cataloging, and so we apply whatever knowledge or stories or myths we have available to explain it."

She was watching me closely, ready to take me down with a ninja response if I made a move for her.

"Have you ever considered that your husband …" I almost couldn't bring myself to say it. I agreed with her. Only a quack would even suggest such a thing. But I was already half in the pond. "Have you considered that your husband might be trying to tell you something?"

She rolled her eyes, recovered, and spat back. "About as likely as me trying to tell him something—since he's six feet under! Good grief, I couldn't tell him anything in life, let alone now!"

"Well, perhaps it's not what he's trying to tell you, but what your subconscious is trying to tell you about him and how you feel, now that he's gone."

She was still giving me the owl's third degree, but I took that as a good sign. At least she was listening. I clasped my hands on the desk, settling in for the long discussion. I felt we might finally be getting somewhere, since clearly there had been a tension between her and her departed husband. This was likely the source of her hallucinations—whether she was willing to recognize it or not.

I opened my mouth to suggest that if she were to consider whether she had fully examined her own feelings about his death…when something caught the corner of my eye.

An elderly man was sitting on my couch, his hands clasped and hanging down between his knees, listening intently, nodding frantically and smiling widely. His eyes, brown and soft, were filled with hope. Overall, he was rather short, somewhat plump and out of shape, his hair grey—well, actually he was a bit grey all over—his face flaccid. Too much good food and spirits, I suspected. He was dressed in somewhat rumpled golfing attire, right down to his grass-stained two-tone golf shoes. His anxious gaze flicked from me to her, back to me, to her…and paused on Mrs. Hillman with what I can only describe as abject adoration.

I choked, coughed, and grabbed my cold cup of coffee from this morning to take a swallow, pushing back from my desk to try to avoid spilling it. Mrs. Hillman watched me without compassion, clearly not impressed. I took two gulps, managed to get my coughing under control, and set it back on the desk with a shaking hand and my eyes firmly fixed on Mrs. Hillman and her obvious disdain.

"Mrs. Hillman, just for the record, what was your husband's name?"

"Norman." She said it with the same asperity as the early Anglo-Saxons would have done when speaking of the invaders who wrested England from their hands. "Norman," she repeated. "I tried to get him to use his middle name—Edward—so much more elegant, but he just couldn't remember to use it." She heaved a sigh of resignation, and shook her head.

I allowed myself to glance at the couch. The man was watching us both intently. I closed my eyes, swallowed hard, and drew a deep breath. When I looked again, Norman smiled at me hopefully. My breath evaporated, but at least my pulse remained stable. I forced my gaze back to Mrs. Hillman.

"How would you describe Norman in life?"

She looked at me as if utterly confused.

"I mean was he a tall man? A pillar of business? Perhaps an athlete?"

She snorted at that and chortled. "Athlete? He could barely manage mowing the yard without stopping to recover halfway through!" She shrugged and patiently responded to me, doing whatever she had to get me to give her that prescription. "He did like golf. Wasn't any good at it, but he liked it, had to have all the things that go with it. We buried him in his golf clothes—silliest thing I ever saw. Those stupid shoes."

I felt my stomach drop a foot—and a surge of sympathy for the man. No wonder he liked a bit of the good stuff now and then. Then I got hold of myself and remembered that I was having an hallucination, having been influenced by Mrs. Hillman and perhaps one too many glasses myself of that excellent wine at last night's banquet. It was past noon. and I had forgone breakfast in favor of two very large, very black coffees, always a bad idea…

I tore my eyes away from Norman and tried Mrs. Hillman's technique. I closed my eyes and determinedly refused to see him. When I looked up, I was immensely relieved to see the couch was empty.

Then I saw my award for last year's charity golf scramble was floating rather languidly toward the window, where it rolled over and twisted around as if someone were examining it closely. My throat tightened. I wasn't sure I could speak.

"Now, look," Mrs. Hillman took control of the session. "I don't know what's going on here or what's wrong with you. If you think you're going to stretch this into two hours for an extra fee—or maybe get me to sign on for more to talk about my 'problem'—you can just forget about it. I'm not crazy, and I don't need any therapy. I just need something to get that fool out of my mind so I can get some sleep!"

"She's always like this when she gets something in her head."

Norman had materialized in the chair next to Mrs. Hillman's. He leaned toward his wife and laid a hand on her forearm. She brushed it off without thinking, like a fly. Norman just sighed, and looked adoringly at her profile then at me with a little shrug.

"I just love the old battle axe. Couldn't live with her, couldn't live without her, you know what I mean?"

He leaned forward and whispered to me conspiratorially.

"You might as well give her what she wants. I always did. It's the only thing that works." He looked down at his shoes a moment. *"I just wanted her to know how much I love her, ya*

know?"

"Yes," I said instinctively, and realized suddenly that Mrs. Hillman had settled back in her chair, finally relaxing.

"All right then. I'll wait while you write the prescription."

"I didn't mean ..." I paused. The hunting heron look returned to her eyes. Norman looked at her and raised a shaggy eyebrow at me.

"Better do it," he said. *"She's got the bit in her teeth now. I mean, what harm can it do, huh?"*

"This drug is very potent, Mrs. Hillman." I leaned back in my chair, realizing suddenly what was happening here. I was obviously feeling intimidated by the woman's sheer power of personality—and I was concerned about the potential consequences if I gave in to her. Perhaps a very small dose or a very limited quantity, just in case she was suicidal and simply refused to seek help for whatever guilt she was carrying. But even so ...

"Well, geez, doc, I mean it wouldn't be that bad if she decided to...ya know...check out early?" Norman looked longingly at his love. *"I don't have anywhere to go without her, and I don't want to be anywhere she isn't ..."*

I couldn't believe I was saying this, or rather that my subconscious was even having this discussion with itself, or ...whatever. This woman was clearly in no hurry to join her husband, and while she was not a spring chicken—I'd guess that both of them were in their late 80's and Mrs. Hillman clearly had the energy and endurance to go the distance—what my subconscious was talking about was condoning suicide, of all things!

I gripped the edge of my desk, appalled, and closed my

eyes, willing Norman to go away—and take my total loss of professional ethics with him! But of course, when I opened them again, he was still there, waiting expectantly, just like Mrs. Hillman. The difference was, he was hopeful, she was furious.

I shook my head and made a decision. "Mrs. Hillman, I believe that I will need to refer you to someone else regarding this prescription." At her look, I plowed through. "I don't feel I can give you this drug with a good conscience. I just don't…I don't fully understand the root cause of your hallucinations and I'm not sure I'm the right counselor for you in this case. I can have my secretary provide you with the names of three excellent alternative practitioners you can contact, but—"

"Oh, for Pete's sake!" Mrs. Hillman stood up and leaned over my desk. "I think you're the one who needs a prescription, or maybe a little vacation—in a padded room. And don't think I'm paying for this so-called session! I'm not paying for talking to a nut case!"

She marched toward the door. Norman watched her a moment, looked back at me with sympathy, and then rose and followed her like a devoted cocker spaniel. He was halfway through the door when she slammed it behind her, and what was left of him just kind of…disintegrated. I heard a brief altercation at Kathy's desk—culminating in Mrs. Hillman's parting remark—"I'd quit if I were you: that man is crazy!"

Half agreeing with her, I sat perched on the edge of my chair for several seconds, waiting, listening, and hesitantly scanning my office with the dread of seeing Norman somewhere… or some object floating in the air. But it appeared that once Mrs. Hillman was gone, he was, too. Feeling somewhat better, I straightened up, drew a rather shaky breath and decided that I needed to get out of this place and put all this behind me.

I'd been working too hard recently, and I had almost let my emotions run away with me. Not something I could afford in my profession. I needed to schedule some time with my own shrink and get to the bottom of this. I wondered if it could have to do with the death of a dear colleague a few weeks earlier, or perhaps the parting several months ago of a decidedly less-than-beloved uncle, whom I had never liked, but who had in the end left me a very nice bequest in his will. Guilt. Yes. Probably guilt.

I waited a good ten minutes, until all seemed quiet on the Western Front. I turned off my computer, locked my desk drawers, and collected a few essentials in my briefcase. I approached the door carefully, and opened it a crack, peering out to make sure she was gone. From across the foyer, Kathy leaned forward at her desk to see me, and smiled knowingly.

"It's okay, she's gone. Whew, what a character!"

"Yes, quite." I crossed the space between us, tugging a little at my tie, and rested my briefcase on the corner of her desk. "Listen, I think I'm going to take a little time off. It's been busy, and I'm not feeling quite up to snuff. I don't think I have anything left today, but would you cancel my appointments the rest of this week? Take a couple of days yourself. We both need a break."

"Well, that would be nice, and I do think you need some time off." She studied my face closely. "Are you really okay?

"Why, don't I look okay?" I managed a smile and swallowed as she cocked her head with a little frown.

"Actually, to tell the truth, you look like you've seen a ghost—kinda pale."

"Ha!" My laugh came out as a rather high-pitched squeak. I managed to shake my head. "No, no, no—just a little too much indulgence last night at the banquet."

"Oh, I know—that wine table was fabulous! My husband finally cut me off at the third glass!" Kathy turned to her computer and pulled up her calendar. "Okay, let's do it. Let's shut down for today and Friday, and I'll see you Monday. Get some rest."

"Actually, I think I might go out to the driving range for a while, hit some balls."

She gave me a thumbs up and set to work, picking up the phone as I moved toward the door to the office and stepped out into the hallway. It was quiet as a tomb, always was in these professional buildings. As I headed toward the stairway, I felt a cold breeze sweep over me.

"So, gonna hit some balls, huh?"

I staggered and fell against the wall. Norman looked embarrassed.

"Hey, doc, I didn't mean to scare you. It's just that, well, she's decided to give up on the drug—you're the second guy who wouldn't give 'em to her—and she's off to the spa for the rest of the day. I hate that place. It's all pink and full of women all chattering away, and I…well, I don't feel right when they get in those massages, you know. 'Sides, when they get that mud on their face, it's downright scary! Maybe I could hang with you for a few hours?"

I pressed against the wall, my hand over my mouth, trying to hold on to my sanity. But I knew what he meant. My second wife used to spend a fortune in those places. Norman nodded as if he heard my thoughts.

"Anyway, hitting some balls sounds great. Which range you go to—that one over by Preston Lake, or that guy with the pro shop out next to the concrete plant? Maybe we could hang out for a few hours, just a couple of golf guys, eh?"

They tell me that Kathy found me on the floor, slumped against the wall, about fifteen minutes later and called an ambulance. They wouldn't let her ride with me, not being family, but Norman was there, assuring me how sorry he was, and that everything would probably be all right—and if it wasn't, he wouldn't leave me.

That's how I ended up at Lone Pine Residency Hospital. My doctor on site said it was probably just a combination of stress from too much work (double alimony is a powerful incentive), a sense of guilt over Uncle Melvin, too much of a bad hobby (the wine club). I didn't bother to tell her that Lone Pine seems to have an unusual number of residual spirits from some previous inmates—eh, patients—who had recovered their senses, but left their ghosts behind. In fact, I've developed rather a new practice talking with the dearly departed who seem to be just about as neurotic as the living. Truth is, I find dead clients a good deal easier to deal with than most of my living ones used to be.

Norman comes to visit occasionally. He feels really bad about the whole thing, but I've assured him, I don't really blame him.

Author's Comments:

I'd already realized after weeks of trying that I simply can't write a scary ghost story. I just have too many years of experiencing too many positive paranormal experiences. Even when I feel a little uneasy in the house, I just send any negative spirits off to seek absolution from Christ and tell them that any spirit of good heart is welcome in my house. But I was puttering around the house when I was struck by the idea that someone might simply refuse to believe they were being haunted—when they really were! I wondered how that works for both the person and the ghost, and those around them. I simply chose a setting where someone might seek help to get rid of a 'delusion.' "Seeing Is Believing" is a whimsical story, rather different from my other styles. But seriously, just because you don't believe in something doesn't mean it isn't real, particularly when it's something you can't really prove or disprove. Just keep that thought in mind some night, when an odd sound, a chilly gust, or a wisp of something white crosses the corner of your eye…and go get your cats and dogs!

The Tunnel
by Chuck Hocter

Prologue

The hill had been there for eons or maybe epochs, certainly for millennia. Had it been created by an upthrust of rock as a result of geothermal pressure? Was it the result of a shifting fault line far beneath the surface in some ancient earthquake? Perhaps it was the rubble left behind by a retreating ice age glacier. Its origin was really unimportant. It was a hill with a heart of stone, covered with rich soil and forest. And it was in the way of progress.

In the year of our Lord 1857, as industry and commerce expanded, transportation became key to further progress. Track had to be laid, trains had to roll, and obstacles such as the hill had to be dealt with—either climbed, skirted, or removed. Climbing the hill would have required too steep a grade. Skirting it would have added far too many miles to the route. And removal—well, removal would have required technology and/or manpower that just did not exist. Thus, the railroad builders were left with only one alternative.

The Tunnel

"Swing them hammers, me boys. Drill that face, lads, so

the night shift can set the charges. Boss man wants to blow this friggin' rock first thing in the mornin'. Can't let them East Boys outdo us. Now get to swingin' them hammers!"

The crew leader's rant was rewarded with a round of hammers striking drills all across the rockface. The sound reverberated off the stone walls and ceiling of the tunnel drowning out the steady drip-drip of water from above. The crew's timing was dead on. The drills reached the required depth just as the quitting bell rang. They gathered up their personal gear and headed for the distant mouth of the tunnel now illuminated by the setting sun. They were the West Crew and they knew they had outpaced the East Boys by at least five feet that day. In total, they figured to be thirty feet ahead in the race to finish the tunnel. Rumor had it the East Boys were trying to catch up by using larger charges and drilling deeper, safety be damned.

That night, as the West Crew set charges for the next day's blow, the East Boys, under orders from their boss, shot the wall with disastrous results. The competition between the two crews had resulted in a serious miscalculation as to how close they were to connecting the two sections of tunnel. The East Boys had taken cover as the crew boss yelled "Fire in the hole!" and lit the fuse. The oversized charge blew through the wall igniting the West Crew's powder and charges, killing three men and seriously injuring the rest of the crew.

The inquiry into the disaster was short and sweet. All blame was placed on the three dead men and the rest were told to get back to work and clean up the mess. After all, there was track to lay and a deadline to meet.

Over the years, tales rose of strange happenings in the tunnel—lanterns burning and no one there, silhouettes of three men in the beam from the locomotive's headlight, sounds of hammers and drills and an occasional muffled explosion. Then there was the westbound freight train, engineer blinded by the setting sun, which hit a wagonload of children on a hayride. Luckily the children had time to jump clear. The train crew wasn't so lucky. Impact with the wagon caused the locomotive to derail which in turn caused the boiler to explode, killing all aboard. People said the tunnel was cursed and eventually the railroad decided the line had outlived its usefulness and closed it down. The tracks were ripped up for use elsewhere or for scrap. Mother Nature reclaimed the land near the tunnel mouths and it was forgotten until ...

Homecoming

Jack pressed the side of his head against the window, peering through the rain-streaked glass, looking for any sign of hope in this dreary storm-soaked day. But there was none to be found. He was riding in the back seat of his father's 1929 Ford Sedan, an unwilling passenger on this trip to a "new life." Jack didn't want a new life. The old one had suited him just fine. Unfortunately, his preferences had meant nothing in the face of the economic collapse that had cost his father his job and house but spared his car. It had been bought with a cash bonus shortly before the crash. So here they were on their way to their ancestral home—actually an abandoned farmhouse, left vacant for years—and their "new life."

"Cheer up, Jack. We're almost there. It's only another mile or so."

His father's voice pulled Jack out of his reverie. He saw that they were crossing an iron bridge over a small creek, the car's tires rumbling on the wood-plank flooring. Just on the other side and running parallel to the creek was an embankment or maybe a dike. It ran for a quarter of a mile or so, straight toward a tall, tree-covered bluff, ending right at its base. Jack's father had been watching him, glancing now and then at the rearview mirror.

"That's the old railroad bed. They tore up the tracks years ago. I think they used the metal to build ships and tanks for the Great War."

That thought caught Jack's attention. He had always had an interest in trains, both toy and real, but something puzzled him.

"Surely the tracks didn't end at the bottom of that big hill, did they?"

"I wouldn't think so, son. More than likely a tunnel was there at one time but it's probably collapsed or been dynamited by now."

Jack turned back toward the window. Too bad about the tunnel, he thought. That would have added some possibility of adventure to what was, in all likelihood, going to turn out to be one big boring mess. Oh well, he'd check it out anyway, first chance he got. He noticed that the rain was slacking off.

A few minutes later, Jack's father turned onto a rutted dirt road and, splashing through mud puddles past two forlorn farmsteads, came to a stop at the dead end before a large two story house that had definitely seen better days. A couple of windows had been boarded up and the lap siding had weathered to a sort of faded gray with, here and there, a stubbornly clinging patch of white paint. No curtains hung in those windows not covered with boards and the image as a whole was one of doom and gloom. The scudding clouds left over from the rainstorm only added to the dismal picture. Jack's mood, already at an all time low, sank even further.

After unlocking the house, unloading the Ford only took a few minutes—three suitcases and a box of groceries. Jack's mom, quiet the whole trip, suddenly turned into a drill sergeant, ordering her husband and Jack around, trying to turn years of abandonment into a habitable space. Dust and cobwebs were everywhere. Fortunately, someone had taken the trouble to cover furniture with heavy drop cloths. And, to everyone's amazement, the rusty old tin roof didn't leak. A chest in one of the upstairs bedrooms yielded enough serviceable sheets and blankets to make up two beds. With a bucket of rainwater, a lot of mumbled curse words, and some dumb luck, Jack's dad got the hand pump out back working. So, after a cold supper of sandwiches and milk, the exhausted trio washed up and fell into bed.

Jack sat bolt upright. It took a moment for him to orient himself. The unfamiliar room around him was dimly lit through the lone window by spillover from a bright beam of light stabbing through the darkness near the old railroad bed. Suddenly one end of the beam erupted in a dazzling light show, followed by the sound of a muffled explosion, then total silence and pitch darkness. Stunned, the boy sat motionless, trying to gather his wits and courage. After a couple of minutes, he slid out of bed and fumbled his way to the window. Looking out, he expected to see fires burning, people running, or some evidence of a huge disaster. There was nothing. The sky was overcast with barely any light from moon or stars and, unlike the city where he used to live, no one here wasted electricity or fuel to keep the area illuminated. Jack slowly found his way back to his bed where he lay wide-awake till dawn.

Jack's parents were totally dismissive of his late-night story. They had neither heard nor seen anything even remotely resembling a train wreck, which was, as Jack later realized, what he had witnessed. His folks just chalked it up to fatigue and his new surroundings. The boy was sure they were wrong but, for the sake of peace, dropped the subject and got back to the effort of reclaiming the old house from more than a decade of neglect. It had last been occupied by Jack's great grandparents on his mother's side. Since her parents were deceased, it had passed down to her. Now it was the only refuge for her family against a world in economic turmoil.

The house had been built around the time of the Civil War by Jack's great-great grandfather. Evidently he had known what he was doing for the house still stood straight and tall and, with the exception of a few broken windows, was still weather-tight. At some point, down through the years, it had been electrified but was presently disconnected from the grid. Candles and kerosene lamps would have to be their light sources for the time being. The house had never had indoor plumbing so there was no worrying about busted pipes. City boy Jack was horrified to learn that he was expected to utilize a little building out back for certain bodily functions. On his first visit, he found it to be infested with spiders and heaven-knows-what down those holes. But, after ridding it of cobwebs and inspecting the space below the holes with a flashlight, Jack grudgingly agreed to use it. However, he knew he would never be comfortable with it.

What the house really needed was a thorough cleaning. Since the weather had cleared, Jack and his father were tasked with moving things outside to be inspected and those items passed by his mother were to be wiped down and returned to the house. And those failing inspection were to be burned or hauled away. While cleaning out a closet on the first floor, Jack came across a box full of photographs, some very old. One of the oldest was a tintype of a young man not much older than Jack's 12 years. He wore a floppy felt hat and what might have been bib overalls—at any rate, work clothes.

"Mom, who's this?"

His mother looked up from the pile of clothing she was sorting, then came and took the picture from him. At first, her face held a puzzled look then relaxed into a slight smile.

"I remember now. This is my great grandfather's youngest brother, John. My Grandpa used to talk a lot about his Uncle Johnny, almost as if they were best friends—which was strange since he never knew him. He died young, before Grandpa was born."

She peered closely at the old picture as if trying to see something in it more clearly. She turned her gaze on Jack. "He looks a good bit like you."

Jack took back the tintype and studied it carefully. He shook his head then tossed the picture back into the box.

"Sorry, I just don't see it. What do you want to do with this stuff?"

"Oh, I guess we'll put them back in the closet for now. When things settle down, I'll go through them and, perhaps, start a family album. Now back to work."

As Jack shoved the box back into the closet, a curious question flashed into his mind, seemingly out of nowhere.

"How did my great-great Uncle Johnny die?"

His mother stopped sorting clothes, her face a study in

concentration.

"You know, I don't believe the cause of his death was ever mentioned, only that he died far too young and was sorely missed. And you left out a great. He was your great-great-great Uncle Johnny."

Jack found that interesting, a puzzle to be solved. While his mind worked on it, he got back to the job of cleaning out the closet, but it held nothing else of particular interest.

As the afternoon wore on, the adults began to move slower and slower till, around three o'clock, they stopped completely and collapsed into a couple of handy chairs. Jack, who should have been exhausted due to lack of sleep, instead felt unusually energized and ready to keep going. His parents gave him jaundiced looks, resenting his youthful vitality. His father spoke up for the two elders.

"Jack, why don't you go explore the area? Your mother and I have run out of steam and need to recuperate. Maybe you can discover what, if anything, it was that woke you up last night."

The boy thought about it for a moment and decided his father was right. Besides, the luster had worn off of the joy of housecleaning.

"Yes, sir! I think that is an excellent idea!"

Jack stood, gave a mock salute and about-faced to leave just as his mother spoke up.

"Be careful and don't do anything foolish and be back here before dark. No telling what may be lurking around here at night."

His mother's warning seemed a bit excessive at first but then Jack took into consideration the events of the previous evening. He had, after all, witnessed a train wreck on a railroad track that no longer existed. Perhaps she had a premonition, he thought. Regardless, his reply came out a bit more sarcastic than he intended.

"I shall be extraordinarily careful and return safely before the stated deadline!"

"Don't be such a smart aleck to your mother, boy. She's only concerned for your welfare in a strange place. Now go before I decide you need a bit more manual labor for exercise."

Jack took the hint. He put on rubber boots to deal with the numerous puddles left over from the previous day's rain. He stood in the yard for a moment, considering his options but there was really only one place he wanted to go. He backtracked on the dirt road till he reached the paved highway. Here the going was easier and in no time the boy had made it to the abandoned railway bed. Jack stared down the length of the embankment, noting that little grass or brush grew on it. At the end of the quarter mile stretch stood the hill— actually more like a tree-covered bluff. Looking at it, Jack felt a chill making him shiver just a bit. He attributed it to the cool breeze blowing in his face, but down deep, he knew it could be something else.

Well, he thought, I've come this far. I might as well press on. Walking along the old rail bed, Jack noticed that the lack of vegetation wasn't the result of mowing. It just looked as if nothing cared to grow there or, perhaps, the weeds and grass were killed off by something passing that way on a regular basis—like, say, a train that wrecked here every so often. The breeze picked up a bit, making a sound almost like whispering. He shivered again but kept going.

"Sean, someone's a-comin'!"

"Ah, Ian, me boyo, ya know there's not a one with guts enough to come around here. They've all larned their lessons."

"Aye, brother dear, but this one's a stranger. Haven't seen him before, though there's something strangely familiar about him."

"Yes, I see it meself. Looks a bit like little John. Speakin' of whom, where is the lad?"

"Outside, more than likely."

"True, true. He doesn't much care for our company. He really shouldn't go out there. It can lead to…complications."

Jack finally reached the base of the hill. The railroad bed ended in a tree line composed of mature hardwoods growing so close together as to form a natural fence. It might as well have had a sign on it reading "KEEP OUT." Naturally this only strengthened his determination to push through and see what was on the other side. So he did. Staying roughly in the middle of the roadbed, Jack struggled and squeezed between the tree trunks, noting that on either side, the ground rose in a rather steep grade while remaining relatively flat in front of him.

After about twenty yards, the trees began to thin out, but only in front of Jack. To his left and right the slope of the hill continued, heavily forested, up and out of sight. Pushing through the last of the brush and trees, Jack found himself staring at what he had hoped to find, a great yawning hole in the hill, soaring to over thirty feet high. His father had been mistaken. The tunnel had neither collapsed nor had it been dynamited. Instead, it stood there, dark, mysterious and inviting—almost as if it were calling his name. For just a moment he thought he could actually hear a soft voice but instead of calling out to him it was singing—a tune that was vaguely familiar. Jack took two steps forward to better hear the song but it ceased abruptly. Suddenly, something pulled him toward the looming darkness, as if he were on an invisible leash. Softly, beginning almost inaudibly, a whisper repeated over and over, "Come in." With each repetition it seemed to come closer, driven by a moist, fetid breeze, becoming coarser and coarser until the last one was the raw tortured plea of a hopelessly trapped soul in bitter anguish. Then silence. The leash snapped and Jack staggered, almost falling. Near the tunnel entrance were several large stones, probably having fallen from the overhang. Jack shakily made his way to one and sat down. He took several deep breaths trying to calm himself and slow his racing heart.

Movement near the mouth of the tunnel caught Jack's attention. What appeared to be a small cloud or a wisp of fog was drifting toward the darkness. As it crossed over from full sunlight to shade, it took on a shape that was vaguely human and glowed. It seemed to be gesturing for Jack to leave, a sentiment with which he completely agreed. Until a few minutes ago, he had intended to explore the tunnel but his recent encounter with a foul-breathed invisible entity had put a damper on his urge to explore. But Jack, even though frightened, was a bit confused. A voice had called to him, had in fact begged him to come in, and now here was an apparition trying to shoo him away. As his breathing and his heartbeat slowed down to nearly normal, he made his decision. He would chase this phantom into the tunnel—at least for a short distance. Curiosity had won out over fear. He just hoped it wouldn't kill him like it had the cat.

This being the west end of the tunnel, the first few feet were lighted faintly by the sun lowering in the afternoon sky. Jack's eyes soon adjusted to the gloom and he could make out details such as rocks, which had fallen from the overhead.

The Tunnel

There was evidence scattered here and there of temporary occupancy by what must have been hoboes and tramps; such things as fire rings and empty tin cans. It didn't appear that anyone had taken up residency recently or for any length of time. Jack surmised that they had only come in seeking shelter from a storm and left, probably in a big hurry when things turned a little weird, such as seeing a man-shaped cloud floating by, like the one he was now chasing deeper into the tunnel. The boy hesitated. He was scared and knew that his parents would soon begin worrying about him, but the need to find out what was going on here was very strong. He gave in and continued his pursuit of the ghostly form.

"Look at that, Sean! Johnny Boy's bringin' that boy in!"

"Aye, Ian, I can see that. This may call for some drastic measures. Do you not recognize the lad?"

"Not sure, though judgin' by his looks, he's some kin to little John. There's more about him that's familiar but I can't quite place it."

"I see what you mean, brother dear, and that's why I called him in! I think he's a Collins!"

"Ah, Sean, me boy, if you're right, maybe sweet revenge is in our grasp at long last!"

Jack had chased his will o' the wisp friend halfway through the tunnel when he needed to stop. He was tired. He had worked all morning, hiked all the way to this point and had the living daylights scared out of him. He needed a break.

The gloom in the tunnel had deepened and Jack noticed that his quarry was becoming a more defined figure. Its features were still too indistinct to form a recognizable face but Jack could tell that it was a boy about his size and age. It seemed to be dressed in old-fashioned work clothes. In fact, it quite resembled the tintype he had seen earlier in the day. While Jack was studying his companion, he thought he heard a distant rumble, followed by the faintest of faint high-pitched sounds—a train whistle. In seemingly no time, the noise became louder and the ground beneath Jack's feet began to vibrate. Then the east end of the tunnel began to glow and a search light beam pierced the darkness.

Jack stood there paralyzed. The apparition at his side grabbed his arm and began dragging him toward the light. Jack struggled to free himself from the ghostly grip but it was too strong at first. Then, with light from the setting sun illuminating the tunnel, his captor became less defined, reverting to his cloud form. He also became weaker, allowing Jack to tear free of his grasp. Jack turned and ran toward the tunnel mouth as the noise behind him increased. Above the tumult, he could hear a frenzied voice screaming.

"Get the Collins! Don't let him escape! We must have our revenge!"

The rumble and the shaking, the whistle and the light were reaching a peak when Jack cleared the mouth of the tunnel. Suddenly, there was near silence, broken only by the sound of leaves rustling in the breeze and the chirping of birds. Jack stumbled to one of the large rocks near the entrance and sat down to catch his breath.

The sun was now very low in the western sky and dusk would soon be upon him, so Jack pushed off from the rock and began the long walk home, his mind a jumbled mass of swirling thoughts and questions. Chief among them was why anyone would want to get revenge on a Collins. Jack was a Collins and, as far as he knew, none of his relatives had ever done anything to deserve the need for revenge. He had lots of questions for his father.

A Little Family History

Jack's Mom had managed to scrape together the ingredients for an actual hot meal instead of just sandwiches. After grace was said, and in between bites, polite conversation began. Jack nervously awaited his chance to bring up relatives. After his parents had reviewed the day to their satisfaction, he saw an opening and took it.

"Dad, do you have any family around here?"

The boy watched as his father's facial expression went from smiling, to puzzlement, to resignation. Wiping his mouth with a napkin, then taking a sip of coffee, his face now under control, the father sat back in his chair and finally answered.

"Not anymore, son. My great grandfather was, at one time, a very prominent member of this community. However, sometime near the middle of the last century, he decided it was time to try his luck in the big city. He was a geologist and an engineer so he had no trouble finding employment. His example inspired both my grandfather and father to follow in his footsteps by becoming engineers. You might say that by becoming an accountant, I'm the black sheep of the family. So the answer to your question is no. To the best of my knowledge, I have no family here. Why do you ask?"

Jack tried to come up with a way to introduce the fact that, apparently, there were some spirits, specters, demons or, maybe, just plain ghosts who had it in for any member of the

Collins Clan. He thought of just blurting out, "I was in the old tunnel today—which by the way, Dad, hasn't collapsed—and some ghosts tried to kill me." But doing that would probably end up with him being banned from ever going near the place again and maybe result in a thorough head examination. He chose another tactic.

"Oh, I don't know, Dad. I just thought since Mom's family was from here, maybe yours was, too."

The father looked across the table at his smiling wife. He began smiling also.

"When I first met your mother, I had no idea of her connection to this place. It was only after we had been married a couple of years and her grandparents passed away that I learned that both our families had deep roots here and most likely had known each other well."

Jack mulled over this large chunk of new information. It seemed that his great-great grandfather on his father's side had decided to leave town at about the same time that his great grandfather on his mother's side was talking about his pal Uncle Johnny who was dead. There had to be a connection. And that connection could possibly be the reason for someone or something seeking revenge on a Collins. Jack ate a few bites and was chewing on a particularly tough piece of meat when another question came to mind.

"Dad, why did your great grandfather leave here? Really?"

His father put down his silverware and stared at his plate, a sour look on his face. After a moment, he looked up and then at Jack, his face now expressionless.

"I had intended to keep this from you until you were much older—or forever. However, our moving here will undoubtedly stir up old controversies among the locals, so you probably should know so as to be prepared. Your great-great grandfather was a mining engineer, especially experienced in shafts and tunnels. When it was decided to run the railroad through here, thus necessitating a tunnel, the company was delighted to find such a qualified individual available locally. As you will no doubt hear, there was a terrible accident in the tunnel we talked about on the way here. Three men were killed and, though the investigation placed the blame for it on the deceased, most folks around here put the blame on my great grandfather, Wendell Collins. When his neighbors became angry to the point of violence, he packed up his family, including my grandfather, and left."

As Jack was taking all this information in, he heard his mother lay down her fork and clear her throat.

"Jack, there's one more fact you need to know. I fibbed a bit when I said great-great Uncle Johnny's cause of death was never mentioned. True, it was never mentioned in the family but I learned from friends that he was one of the three killed in the great tunnel explosion."

The boy took a couple of bites of his supper, chewing the food as his mind digested all that he had just been told. One question bobbed to the surface almost immediately.

"Who were the other two victims?"

His father shrugged his shoulders and shook his head but his mother answered.

"Those would be the Rafferty brothers, Sean and Ian. From the stories I have heard, they were troublemakers, rough and rowdy and not nice at all. They came from a large family who led the group blaming Wendell Collins for the explosion. They tried to sue the railroad but couldn't afford competent lawyers and got nothing for their trouble. So, like the Collins family and my family, the Gilhoolys, they gradually all died out or moved away."

The conversation lagged after that and everyone concentrated on eating. Jack kept rerunning his afternoon's adventure, trying to fit this new information into it and make some sense of it, but success eluded him. After supper, he feigned fatigue and went to his room. There he stretched out on his bed, fully clothed, to continue the review of his day. He must have been more worn out than he thought for he promptly fell asleep.

Revenge

Jack was back in the tunnel with the train approaching and someone dragging him toward it by the arm. His vision cleared and he could see that it was Uncle Johnny doing the dragging.

"Why are you doing this? Why do you want to kill me?"

Now fully solid and in focus, Johnny turned toward him. The ghost's tintype face full of determination and sadness.

"I'm not trying to kill you! I'm trying to save you! You must trust me."

Suddenly, everything dissolved in the glaring light of the approaching train and Jack found himself lying on his bed in total darkness. He sat up and began fumbling for matches to light a candle.

"Don't make a light, Jack."

A shiver ran down Jack's spine. The voice sounded as if it came from deep in the tunnel, an echo vibrating slightly, and unreal.

"Who's there?"

"In life I was John Gillhooly. Do you know the name, perhaps?"

Jack had suspected that the wraith he had encountered at the tunnel was his great-great-great uncle. His mother's naming him as one of the victims of the great explosion had made it almost certain. This made it even more confusing as to why Johnny had tried to kill him.

"Yes, I know your name. There's a picture of you in a down-stairs closet."

"I know the one. It's the only likeness of me. It was made shortly before the day of the explosion."

"So, great-great-great Uncle, why do you want me dead?"

Johnny's answer came swiftly, in a voice both shocked and confused.

"But Jack, I want no such thing! Whatever gave you an idea of that sort?"

"Well, there's the fact that you tried to drag me into the path of a speeding freight train."

When Johnny answered, his voice was subdued and hurt.

"Is that what you thought, then? That I was trying to kill you? I was trying to save you! There is an alcove carved into the side of the tunnel for just that purpose, if someone should meet with a train while walking through. That's where I was dragging you to."

Silence filled the darkness of Jack's bedroom. He considered Johnny's explanation and found it plausible. He wanted to look upon his ancestor's face and began once more to search for a match.

"Please don't light a candle. I need the darkness. It is my strength and we'll both be needing that this night."

Jack didn't like the way that sounded—as if they were

going into battle and he wasn't sure he was ready for it.

"Alright, Uncle. What's up?"

Jack could almost hear the smile in Johnny's voice as he answered.

"Jackie, me boy, we are going to confront the Rafferty brothers, stare them down and deny them the one thing, maybe the only thing, they have desired for the last eighty or more years."

"And that would be?"

"Revenge."

The trek through the darkness was a painful experience for Jack. He lost count of how many times he stubbed his toes or barked his shins. Johnny, unfazed and apparently floating several inches above all obstacles and tripping hazards, kept insisting that he needed the darkness. When finally they reached the tunnel, they found it bathed in a soft glow with enough light inside to show them the way. Jack looked at Johnny, the question on his lips, but Johnny beat him to the punch.

"This is not natural light and there's no time to explain the difference. We must hurry. It will be daybreak soon."

Jack, following the floating Johnny, trudged down the track toward the halfway mark of the tunnel. There he and Johnny found the Rafferty brothers, waiting, scowling, and definitely not in a good mood.

"Well, Little John, I see you've brought the Collins."

"Wrong, Sean, I've brought the Gillhooly!"

"Aye, Johnny, he's a Gillhooly, but first and foremost, he's a COLLINS! And we'll be takin' our revenge on him."

Jack could see the rage starting to build in the faces of both

Raffertys. Johnny, on the other hand, stood calm and stone-faced as if in the eye of a hurricane. Jack knew that Johnny thought he had the upper hand, but he himself wasn't so sure.

"So, Sean, tell me. If Jackie, here, was a Rafferty instead of a Gillhooly, would you be so keen to take out your revenge on him?"

"Such a silly question, lad. Of course I wouldn't harm family. But, then, he isn't a Rafferty, is he?"

"Are you so sure of that? Come closer. Look into his eyes. Touch his hand."

Jack stiffened and closed his eyes as the now furious Sean came toward him. He could feel the coldness radiating from him as he leaned near and then the shock of his touch.

"What tomfoolery is this? He can't be kin! He's a Collins! But I feel the presence of family. How can this be? How can he be a Rafferty?"

"Things can change over the years, Sean. Not everything gets passed down from generation to generation. My own great-great niece married a Collins."

Sean's face reflected his inner turmoil. Anger, frustration and hate chased each other across his visage. But then a thought came to him and all was replaced by determination.

"Of course! The only explanation is that somewhere down the years, a Rafferty married a Gillhooly, makin' this one kin. But his father has no such protection. Ian, come. We're goin' outside to hunt down a Collins!"

"No, Sean! You and Ian will be goin' nowhere. There are no Raffertys in my family tree. Over the years, I've often visited outside this tunnel and tried to keep track of the goings on there. Now listen carefully to what I've learned. Ian, when you died, you left behind a young wife and infant daughter. The wife remarried and

her new husband, an O'Leary, adopted the daughter. The daughter, in due time, married a Dogherty and had a daughter who married a Flannigan. He was an ambitious young man who took his wife off to the city to seek his fortune."

At this point, Jack suddenly perked up. He looked from Johnny to Sean to Ian.

"No, it can't be. My grandmother, my father's mother, her maiden name was Flannigan. Ian, that makes you my great-great grandfather!

"Actually, Jack, you left out a great. But you get the idea. You are a Collins. You are also a Gillhooly on your mother's side and a Rafferty on your father's side. So now, Sean, what are you going to do?"

Sean Rafferty, who in life had been a huge man, now began to grow even larger. His face, which had always seemed flushed, became even darker till he was nearly the color of blood. Jack, Johnny, and even Ian began to back away from him. And in the distance could be heard the whistle of a train soon followed by the roar of the engine at full speed and the vibrations of the ground from the wheels on the uneven tracks.

"No-o-o-o-o-o, I will have my revenge! I will not be denied!

The beacon from the headlight of the phantom locomotive pierced the darkness of the tunnel, casting four silhouettes on the tunnel walls, frozen in place. At nearly the last moment, Ian seized Sean and they struggled toward the onrushing train.

"No, Sean, they're my blood! I must protect them!"

While the Raffertys struggled in the glaring light, Johnny grabbed Jack by the arm and rushed to the side of the tunnel and fell into the alcove in the rock. They hit the damp floor just as the ghostly train sped by outside the niche. Sparks and lightning bolts shot from the wheels, narrowly missing the two huddled inside. After the last car passed, the sound of a huge explosion rocked the tunnel, then—silence.

Johnny recovered first and helped Jack to his feet. They exited the alcove, only to find no sign of a train wreck or the Raffertys. Jack turned to his companion, his expression begging for an explanation.

"Well, nephew, that should take care of that. Sean and Ian are gone and probably won't return. With the possibility of getting revenge taken from them, they have no reason to be here. Unlike them, I have a connection to this place that doesn't require violence and bloodshed. I may stay a while and keep track of my kinfolk. You, young John Thomas Collins—you were named after me, you know—have a life to lead now that the death sentence has been lifted. So, go."

Jack watched as Johnny began to fade in the light of the sun rising at the east end of the tunnel. He tried to touch the now nearly transparent figure but in vain. Johnny smiled.

"We'll meet again, now and then. Just listen and you'll hear me. There's a song I like that the boys brought home from the Great War. Perhaps you know it."

Johnny disappeared and Jack could hear him whistling a familiar tune—the same tune he had heard on his first visit to the tunnel. He began whistling along and started down the old railroad bed toward home. Then he began singing.

"There's a long, long trail a-winding to the land of my dreams ..."

Epilogue

A young man, wearing the neatly pressed uniform of an Army Lieutenant, limped down the old railroad bed toward the tree line at the base of a large hill, almost a bluff, really. Working his way through the trees he came to what had once been the entrance to a tunnel. It was now collapsed, the result of an earthquake or, as some swore, an explosion in the middle of the night, almost like a train wreck.

The young soldier stared at the pile of massive rocks sealing the tunnel, probably forever.

"I made it back, Johnny. A sniper tried to take me out but only got a piece of my leg. They say it'll get better in time. I had hoped to come in and see you again but that's impossible now. But you know, I still think about you and the great debt my family owes you. Be at peace, John Thomas Gillhooly. You've earned it."

Jack turned away and somewhere deep in the bowels of the hill, he could hear someone faintly whistling.

"I hear you, Uncle Johnny."

Then he walked away, singing as he went..

"There's a long, long trail a-winding …"

Author's Comments

About a quarter mile from the house I grew up in, there was a railroad crossing and a tunnel through a hill. Part of growing up, a rite of passage if you will, was to walk through the tunnel alone—a distance of about two or three hundred yards. This was an active tunnel so the danger was from real trains, not ghosts. Later, after the railroad was closed and the tunnel was abandoned, my sister and her husband used it to grow mushrooms. Not very scary but interesting, I thought.

The Boy with No Name
by John Hanford

From her car Marilyn Huber saw other grandparents stream into the one-story limestone St. Patrick Catholic School. St. Pat's was hosting its annual Grandparents Day. The October morning was breezy, the autumnal colors vivid. The fluttering leaves heightened the festive mood. After she parked, Marilyn walked quickly and gabbed with another grandmother as they entered. She looked forward to seeing her grandchildren, Maddie, seven, and Owen, eight. They were her youngest. Today she would again have the chance to be part of their growing lives.

Since her husband's death, Marilyn had taken too few opportunities to feel the joy of her grandchildren. She was grateful that her daughter-in-law, Kathryn, had prodded her into participating. She felt guilty it took Kathryn's pushing to get her involved. Marilyn had discontinued much of her family time since Henry's death almost four years ago. Although an accomplished professional, Henry Huber's existence pivoted around family as was also the case with Marilyn.

Inside the front doors, children's artwork festooned the large hall that served as the morning gathering area and cafeteria. The grandparents were ushered by older students into the gymnasium where there were neat rows of folding chairs. The grandparents smiled and the fifth grade ushers beamed as they received compliments. Anticipation welled up. The school hummed with last minute preparations for the student presentation. Marilyn found an end seat a couple of rows back from the front. Children were busy throughout the gym. A little girl in a black and white houndstooth dress with red tights caught Marilyn's attention. How darling is that!, she thought. From her side she noticed a child approaching.

Marilyn turned to see a pale child wearing baggy, brown-corduroy pants and an old-style plaid sweater. Marilyn thought him to be Owen's age, maybe a year older. Once the boy saw Marilyn looking at him, he smiled and ran the last few feet to her.

"Hi, Grandma." The boy appeared to be searching Marilyn's face.

"Well, hi there, honey. I'll be glad to be your grandma today if she's not here. What's your name?" Marilyn's friendly demeanor put children at ease.

At hearing this, the boy's smile grew. Marilyn noticed he resembled her son, Robert, when he was nine. Marilyn recognized Robert's features in this little face, but there was something else she could not identify.

"Grandma, you are my grandma." The little boy was incredulous the way nine year-olds get when something so obvious eludes comprehension by adults. This tripped Marilyn's grandmotherly instincts.

"What's your name, honey?" Marilyn asked with a smile to reassure.

"I don't have a name. I wasn't given one." The smile on his face faded as he looked at the floor.

Marilyn stood as apprehension replaced her excitement.

She hugged her little companion. Marilyn released him when she realized the boy felt cold.

"Sorry to scare you, Grandma. I know I'm cold, but I don't feel it."

Marilyn felt the boy's forehead; it was frigid. Her apprehension grew into vague dread.

"Do you love me, Grandma?" The little boy's face pleaded.

"Honey, where's your teacher? We should get you to the nurse."

Upon hearing this, the boy turned and ran off. As he was about to disappear around a corner he looked back at Marilyn and shouted, "I love you, Grandma."

Concerned the boy was sick, Marilyn walked quickly to catch him. As she rounded the corner, she was met by a dead-end. The boy had vanished. Marilyn became dizzy and a faint wind-like roar filled her head. She was unsteady as she weaved back to her seat. Another grandmother noticed her distress.

"Are you alright, dear?"

"The little boy. He ... he just left."

"He was adorable in those old-fashioned clothes and that curly hair. Is he your grandson? Can I get you some water?"

Marilyn perked up. "So you saw him. You saw the little boy talking to me."

"I did. I'll just grab a glass of water, dear."

Marilyn slumped back, relieved that she hadn't been seeing things. She was confused by the boy's familiarity with her, his insistence she was his grandmother, and his disappearance. The implications of this encounter were featureless forms racing about her mind.

"Oh dear. Oh my ..." Marilyn made the sign of the cross. That's when Maddie ran up with a big hug.

Marilyn's hands trembled on the steering wheel. She was at a loss what to do. What happened at St. Patrick's didn't make sense. She knew to call Patricia Parisi, her best friend since kindergarten. Marilyn and Tricia were life partners in a way, both seventy-six years old and widows. Each had been in the other's life longer than practically anyone else. The thought of hearing Tricia's familiar voice calmed her.

As soon as she arrived home, Marilyn rang up her friend. "When I got around the corner, he was not there. There was only a brick wall. I nearly fainted on the spot." Marilyn clenched the phone tighter.

"Did anyone else see this boy?"

"Yes, another grandmother told me she saw him. You would have died seeing the look on his little face when he said he didn't have a name."

"Have you told anyone else?"

"No. Neither Owen nor Maddie were in the gym yet. And I'm afraid to tell my kids. What if they think I'm senile and won't let me see the grandchildren anymore? They wouldn't do that, would they?" Before Patricia could respond, Marilyn continued, "I know I've not spent time with family like I did when Henry was here." Henry and Marilyn had been married for forty-four years. "And when I finally do, this crazy thing happens. If the kids don't think I'm senile, they'll think I'm nuts."

"Marilyn Huber, you aren't crazy or senile, and spending more time with the kids would lift your spirits. Goodness knows you need that. This is different." Tricia's speech slowed and her voice grew quieter. "Listening to you talk about the little boy makes the hair on the back of my neck stand on end. There's something else going on here. Kids don't just disappear from sight like that." Patricia, the pragmatist, offered a suggestion. "I think you should talk to Monsignor. He's Jesuit; he's smart. All those Jesuits are smart. He can help you sort this out. I'll go with you if you want."

Patricia was referring to the cleric who had formerly been the pastor of their parish. Ed Shinskie was now the Vicar General of the Kansas City-St. Joseph Diocese. He was second to the bishop in rank. Both women respected and trusted this man. He had a presence that suggested spiritual authority.

"I don't know. He must be so busy now. I'll pray tonight." It was Marilyn's way to delay a decision.

"You need to talk to Kathryn, too. You're worried about her knowing, but she's as close as any daughter. She's aware you're not crazy."

"I don't know if I can speak to Kathryn about this. I just don't know."

Shortly after Marilyn got off the phone, she did not care for having two decisions to make. So, she made one: to talk with Monsignor Shinskie. If nothing else, just talking to him could be comforting. She picked up the phone again and scheduled an appointment.

The secretary's manner was bureaucratic and less than spiritual, but Marilyn was pleased to know she would speak with Monsignor Shinskie within the week.

After her rosary and before sleep, Marilyn had another conversation.

"Why did you do this? What do you want of me? This poor little boy was so out of place...so lost." However, she could not continue. The memory of the boy becoming downcast when he told her he had no name brought tears.

Marilyn fell into a fitful night's sleep and awoke exhausted. This continued for the next five nights leading to Tuesday.

She had spoken about the event to no one besides Tricia. She looked forward to receiving clarity from the Monsignor; perhaps he could suggest a course of action that would alleviate her anxiety. Maybe then she would talk to Kathryn about the nameless boy. Marilyn also dreaded this appointment. Being raised in the old traditions of Catholicism, she felt as if she could be telling someone who might cast judgment.

The morning of Marilyn's appointment was overcast, the air chilled. Set against the gray clouds, the gold-leaf neo-baroque dome of the Cathedral of the Immaculate Conception shone like a beacon. The diocesan offices were located adjacent to the cathedral. The familiar sight of the cathedral's dome did not quell Marilyn's misgivings. What if the little boy had been a student? After all, he was a child in a school full of children. The unearthly chill to the child was unusual, but not impossible. Marilyn thought that perhaps she was just a sentimental, foolish old woman; this added to her doubt whether or not to share the story with the Monsignor.

She entered the cathedral sanctuary to pray for strength and calm. In spite of her misgivings, the reason Marilyn proceeded with the appointment had nothing to do with logical thinking. She knew this little boy was a lost soul. She certainly couldn't prove it, but she thought this is what the church is based upon: faith, the firm belief in that which cannot be observed or proven but is indeed true and real.

It took a moment for Marilyn's eyes to adjust to the dimness of the cathedral. Once she could see, she took in a church she had not looked upon before. She had attended masses here when it was full and well lit. Now this was an empty space with soft light filtered through stained glass and possessed the type of quietness only large empty spaces produce. Marilyn sensed a solemn energy filling all the emptiness so that it no longer seemed hollow but perfect for reflection and prayer. She felt reassured.

As she walked to a pew she noticed a young man exiting the altar area; she assumed he was a priest. He made eye contact, passed by, and bid Marilyn good morning. She immediately noticed his radiantly attractive good looks. Marilyn didn't associate the concepts of "handsome" and "priest." To her they were all just priests. She located a pew facing a large statue of the Blessed Virgin. She knelt there and beseeched her namesake to intervene on her and the little boy's behalf. After her prayers, Marilyn headed off to her appointment.

The secretary showed Marilyn into the Vicar General's office. Monsignor Shinskie stood from behind his desk, greeted her, and sat back down. He gestured for Marilyn to sit in one of the chairs facing his desk. They engaged in preliminary talk recalling the days when he had been her pastor. Then they began.

"So tell me, Marilyn, why have you come to see me today?"

Marilyn could not believe that the secretary with no personality had not informed the Monsignor.

"I was under the impression you already knew. When I made the appointment I told ..."

"Yes, Marilyn. My secretary shared with me your conversation. However, I need to hear it from you, in your own words."

Marilyn told the Monsignor everything as she remembered it. She finished and leaned back in her seat, exhausted with a headache. The Monsignor handed Marilyn a thick book. He then referred to sheets of paper on his desk.

"Marilyn, this book contains the Church's policies on apparitions. The earliest policies originated from the 25th Council of Trent in the 16th century. The latest Papal Letters date from 1966 and 1978. In order to prove that a vision is supernatural, the Church has strict protocols. One involves a thorough investigation into the reporter's mental status, character, and motivation for coming forward. The church requires this before any aspect of the appearance is considered. This is the only way I can proceed further with this matter. Are you sure this is something you want the Church to go forward with?"

"I don't know. I'm not sure..."

"Well then, Marilyn, what is it you want from the Church?"

Marilyn thought she hadn't wanted anything from the Catholic Church. She only wished for the counsel of a trusted priest.

"I just want you to tell me what to do."

"Marilyn, this 'visit' happened in a school building full of children. You spoke to a child." The Monsignor made parenthetical signs with his fingers as he uttered "visit." Shinskie then shrugged, "My recommendation is... to pray. You can't go wrong with prayer. God will let you know if he needs anything from you."

"Monsignor, I..."

"Yes?"

"Thank you so much for your time, Monsignor."

"You are quite welcome. Please say hello to your children for me."

Unnoticed by Marilyn, the secretary had stepped in and stood at her side to escort her out.

Marilyn was queasy and walked the short distance to the

cathedral sanctuary to regain her composure.

As she entered, Marilyn sat in a pew, closed her eyes, and made a conscious effort to slow her breathing. She could not yet unravel her feelings regarding what just happened. Marilyn let out an angry sigh. She wasn't sure if her anger was at Monsignor Shinskie because of his lack of empathy and generic advice or at herself for getting carried away in such foolish a notion as a little lost soul reaching out to her.

"Marilyn, you foolish, lonely old woman. What did you expect with such a cockamamie fairy tale," she scolded. Marilyn slumped for a moment then began to gather her things. As she stood, she noticed the young man she had seen earlier standing at the end of the pew.

"You look troubled. Perhaps I can help." He offered a smile meant to calm.

"Father, I don't mean to be rude, but I think it best I just go. I've not done very well with the clergy today."

"Please. I believe I can help. That's why I'm here. Tell me what you need of God. I'll believe you." His smile was warmth.

Marilyn thought it odd for this priest to say that he would believe her. He had not heard the story. But she could tell he was earnest.

"Please don't judge me, Father." This was more a plea than request.

"I've not been sent to judge. I only want to help."

Marilyn sat back down. He sat next to her and had the aroma of the incense burned in Catholic churches. Marilyn thought perhaps he could have said mass earlier, but he was not wearing clerical clothing. When he turned to look at her, she read in his face that it would be safe to tell her story.

Marilyn told him everything. She even shared the

condescending manner in which the Monsignor had treated her and the church protocol he proposed. The young man kept eye contact and exuded peaceful composure.

"I have faith in you," he said. "Our protocol shall be to talk. That's all." Marilyn nodded her acceptance of this.

"Have you lost anyone, especially children or grandchildren?"

Marilyn told him she had not. She did not believe her daughter-in-law had lost children. She mentioned Henry's death four years ago.

"Marilyn, by 'lost' I don't mean only through death. Perhaps someone has lost their way or become distant."

Marilyn nodded that she understood. "No, Father, no one that I can think of has become lost in that manner."

"You said he resembled someone close. Please tell me about that."

"He bore a resemblance to my son Robert when he was a boy. My grandson Owen, Robert's boy, looks like his dad. Father, there was something else familiar in that little fella's face. Try as I might, I couldn't figure out what it was."

"I can see you're anguished. Please tell me why this visit has caused this. Again, I can see it. I want to hear your words, so I'll know how to offer the best help." The man shifted so that he directly faced Marilyn.

"Father, I could sense this boy needed love, he needed to be loved, and he wanted me as his grandma to love him. If this child is at a place where I can make a difference to him, I need to do that. He reached out to me, Father. When he told me he had never been given a name, it broke my heart. I could see all the rejection this little one felt, the terrible pain. It's not right for children to feel so badly." Marilyn began to tear up. "Please tell me what to do." Marilyn's tension increased to sobbing.

The priest took her hands into his. This comforted her.

"Marilyn, look at what this boy said he needed. He told you, and you heard him. He said he needed a grandmother's love. He said he needed you as his grandmother. He asked for your love. What do you feel you should do? It's not what you **think** you should do. Do what you **feel**. If you follow your instincts, he shall not want again."

"But, father, what if this child is out there somewhere? What if he has no one to care for him?"

"What you feel is where you should look. This is wisdom that does not come from thought or can be given by another. You've prayed about it, and you have your answer. Search within to see it." He stood and bent slightly to look Marilyn in the face. "This boy came to the right person for the right reason. You are a wonderful being, full of love. Share this gift with him and all your grandchildren. In the end it will be as it should be. You will know peace and joy." The man gently released Marilyn's hands and turned to leave.

Marilyn smiled. "Father, thank you so much. I don't even know your name."

"Thank you for being open to my help. That is why I came. I'll always be nearby." As he turned, Marilyn glanced down at the hankie in her hand. When she looked up toward the man, he was gone. She shifted to catch a glimpse of him as he walked down the side aisle of the sanctuary. However, there was no sign of him in the now serene cathedral.

Indian summer felt glorious after a week of gray skies and bluster. It had been that long since Marilyn's visit to the cathedral. She had prayed to find meaning in the little boy's appearance and searched within where the priest assured her she would find answers. Peace and joy, however, were nowhere in her heart.

She was on her way to Kathryn's house. Kathryn had researched the Huber family history at the Midwest Genealogy Center in Independence and said she had found something quite interesting about Henry. Marilyn couldn't imagine what it was. Kathryn insisted her mother-in-law visit her so she could share the news in person.

"Did Maddie enjoy that I came to her school?" Marilyn asked as she took off her jacket.

"Of course she did, Mom, though she did say you were a bit distracted," Kathryn said.

"Distracted?" Marilyn sounded incredulous.

"She didn't use that word. She said you kept looking around as if someone else was going to show up. She loved taking you around to her classroom. Loved it." Kathryn hoped she had defused any annoyance Marilyn felt.

"It was fun, honey. Thank you for encouraging me to go." Marilyn emphasized the word *encouraging*.

"Well, Mom, we all miss that you haven't felt up to things like that." Kathryn's concern was apparent.

"Okay, Kath, what have you found out about the Hubers?" Marilyn deflected. She was curious about what could have possibly been found out about Henry's family. Henry was adopted as a nine year-old by the Hubers. There was no prior family history.

Kathryn showed her mother into the dining room and gave her a Diet Coke, Marilyn's preferred daytime drink. She opened the curtains, allowing the sunny autumn colors to fill the room. The daughter-in-law sat next to Marilyn to give her the news.

Kathryn explained she had located the orphanage where Henry had been adopted. It was the German Orphan Asylum in Washington, D.C. Because the institution was of historical interest, its documents were digitally preserved. Kathryn was able to gain the information about her father-in-law through the Internet.

As an infant, the boy first arrived at the orphanage in a wicker basket left outside the front door. Orphanage paperwork indicated he arrived with no documentation or name. The orphanage assigned this inmate the number 71, meaning he was the seventy-first child in residence. The orphanage staff began to call Inmate 71 Heinrich. Jacob and Margarethe Huber adopted Inmate 71 in 1943.

Marilyn gasped.

"I know!" Kathryn said. "Isn't that wild that they called the children inmates? Can you imagine?"

"No, honey. I can't believe he was not given a name. He was a number."

"Well, thank goodness the staff called him Heinrich. Grandma and Grandpa changed his name to Henry," said Kathryn. She knew it was inappropriate to modern sensibilities to call children inmates and number them. But Kathryn was unable to grasp the full impact it made on Marilyn that Henry had arrived at the orphanage with no name.

"Kathryn, Henry's parents Americanized 'Heinrich' to 'Henry.' That's what immigrants did back then." Marilyn spoke the words with a far-off look. Then she smiled.

With authority Marilyn stated, "We're doing Thanksgiving at home this year, my house. Please let everyone know."

"How wonderful. What a nice surprise."

"Honey, we've both had great surprises today." With that

Marilyn kissed her Kathryn goodbye and began to plan the holiday.

Thanksgiving Day aromas spiced Marilyn's home. This was the first Thanksgiving there since Henry had passed. The sounds of laughter from those she loved filled her heart. Her family, all the children and grandchildren, were there, six grandchildren from sixteen to seven in age. Marilyn and her daughters-in-law were busy ferrying dishes of food from the kitchen to the dining room table. Kathryn issued orders for everyone to gather. The much anticipated feast was ready.

Children began to assemble; the fathers cast looks to settle them down. The family tradition was to gather around the table to say grace and give thanks before sitting. Marilyn removed her apron and told Robert she would be leading the prayer this year.

Marilyn began by crossing herself, "In the name of the father…" Everyone followed her lead.

"Heavenly Father, this family is so very grateful that once again we can gather together to give thanks and celebrate our good fortune: health for all, each other's love, all of this made possible by Your love. These gatherings will be wonderful memories for all of us. We all wish Henry could also be here, but he is in our hearts and we feel his presence. Thank you for that, Father."

A surge of anticipation coursed through the older grandchildren as they knew mention of Grandpa Henry was the last part of the blessing before they could enjoy all the food spread before them. The smell of dinner rolls still in the oven intensified their hunger. To their surprise Marilyn continued.

"Today, Father, we have another gift to be thankful for."

A few glanced at each other. William, the oldest grandchild, shrugged at his sister's puzzled look.

"Our Heavenly Father recently reminded me of a little boy I used to know. He is in the same warm place as Grandpa." When Maddie gave Marilyn a questioning look, she said, "He is in heaven, dear." She continued. "The little boy helped me remember that I'm most happy when I'm surrounded by my beautiful grandchildren and our wonderful family. We are so very warm and loving with each other. Henry showed me that we always have room in our hearts for more love and joy. Thank you, Heavenly Father, for allowing me to see this anew and with such clarity. Amen."

The family sat down to a feast filled with laughter and love. The entire family gathered to enjoy each other's company and give thanks. Marilyn surveyed the scene with peace and joy. That night after prayers and before sleep Marilyn addressed Henry. "Dear, I don't know if that was you that day in the school. I followed my heart and did the best I could. I'll keep at it. If it wasn't you, please look after that little boy. Even if it was you, love him as a grandfather. Just as you needed a grandpa, Henry, so might he."

––––––––––––

The German Orphan Asylum was established in 1880 with facilities completed in 1890. It was located on Good Hope Road in southeast Washington, D.C. In early 1964, a developer offered to rent the property for 99 years at a price that allowed the orphanage to relocate. The facilities at that location were later demolished. The glorious turn-of-the-century brick building that housed up to eighty children, or inmates as the orphanage referred to them, is now part of Washington's obscured history. The orphanage relocated to Prince Georges County, Maryland and closed its doors to children in 1978. It is now an assisted-living facility. Lost Washington D.C and greatergreaterwashington.org are two resources for discovering the lost history of Washington, D.C.

Author's Comments:

The first scene of this story simply came to me almost in its entirety. I merely had to fill in the details, such as the child not having a name. I wasn't sure where the story would lead; the writing and revision process worked that out for me. I'm not sure if there were any underlying conditions or events in my life that provided the inspiration to write this story; however, the ultimate message of reconnection may have influenced me. I used The Cathedral of the Immaculate Conception in Kansas City, Missouri, as the location of Marilyn's visit for assistance from the Monsignor and her encounter with the individual in the sanctuary that eventually helped her.

The postscript about the orphanage that numbered the children rather than name them is something I stumbled across on the Internet as I searched for institutions that did not give names to the children under their care.

Bringing Them Home
by R.M. Kinder

When his parents were surely asleep, Tim quietly slipped outside. Moonlight made the world very visible but slanted, shadows and flickers moving and not truly recognizable. He closed the gate behind him. The vet's place was only minutes away by car, so he could walk there and be back before his parents were up.

Their yard had been the territory of three companions: Caspar, humongous, black-and-white lazy pool of cat, Saturday, a tiny gray leaping and zooming cat, always displaying skills for Tim, who would cheer and applaud, "Go! Atta cat!" Both cats had died over a year ago. And now Zeke, a small, golden, fierce ratter dog, who should have lived to be Tim's age at least, but had died at six years. Last week. Because someone left the gate open.

When Tim asked his mother if animals went to heaven, she said, "Probably not. Animals don't have souls and souls are what ascend to heaven."

"Where do ghosts go?"

"They're supposed to hang around until someone helps them move on to heaven."

"Helps them how?"

"Honey, honey." Which was her way of sending love when unable to do more. "Whatever they need, you know? Answer a question or find something. Maybe they're afraid. But Tim, honey, ghosts are more a story than fact."

As far as Tim was concerned, God, the Devil, Angels, and Ghosts were equal. Unseen.

Six blocks of houses and businesses, then up a hill past the park and down a two-lane road with high trees on either side, the moon vast and close overhead. Two cars appeared but Tim just darted a few feet away and squatted low, like one of the creatures who often died crossing roads.

Then the vet's place. One weak glow at the entrance and another at the back. A wooden, broad-slat fence ran the length of the lot. Tim climbed it, sat where he could see the side and rear of the clinic. In there, animals were "put down," his dad said, as kindness when they were ill or terribly injured. Then the bodies were disposed of. Gone off the earth. "Sorry," Tim said, for about the millionth time in his life.

He held very still, but watched and listened intently. At first he heard nothing but the distant, strange animal roar that cars made, at night, and a huge silence that was itself the sound of waiting, full and whole. Tiny shadows like moths flitted around the lights. A bird took off from the roof. Tim didn't know birds flew at night. Or if they slept. He wasn't certain of anything. He shifted position, and the visible light wavered, rippled. He turned his head quickly and the light streaked into the shadows, shattered. Everywhere outlines blurred, depths and shapes appeared, moving. The tree leaves shimmered. He heard birds, faint whee-ets, twirps, trills. "Zeke," he whispered. "Zeke," louder.

He jumped down from the fence, going toward the

sometimes-grassy patch alongside the building. All sounds but his had now ceased. How could any creature remain? Maybe for a little while, at least. His chest hurt. He didn't know what to do. He couldn't leave without knowing where they were. All of them. Just to know! He knelt as he would have at home. "Zeke! Caspar! Saturday!" He patted his thighs. "Come! I'll take you someplace good."

He felt their presence. His body and mind knew. He didn't have to see them as he once had. Here they were, sparks of light and pools of darkness, curling this way and that. They had waited. He gathered them in, stroking, felt the tingle of limbs he could almost see. Of course they had souls. And where his went, theirs went. He stood up. "We're leaving."

He talked the whole way, cried a little. "You don't have to worry about where to go now. You can hang around with me. I can help when I know more. So don't go. You must stay with me." He worried he might lose them on the way, because they never travelled this far without being in a car. He told them how much he missed them, said their names often.

Approaching the back gate, he could feel their excitement. Zeke had surely run ahead and was nosing the gate for someone to open it, hurry, hurry. "Got it," Tim said, holding it open for a few seconds before closing it. "You don't have to go anywhere." Their delight was visible, the yard warm and bright, soothing, slowing them down and him, too. He went up the steps to the back deck and sat down in one of the chairs. He was very happy being near his parents, his room. He knew there were more creatures unseen than seen. Maybe there was a ghost of everything loved. That would be heaven. Not just cats and dogs, even, but birds, turtles, moons, trees, rivers, flowers. He was so filled with the wonder of knowing that he couldn't go to bed, but fell asleep in good company, deeply comforted.

Author's Comments:

Some people believe that humans have souls but animals do not. As a child this troubled me. I gradually decided to believe that heaven would be the continued existence of what a person loves. That chosen belief and my love of animals (too limited a word for all they are) led me to this story, which is my favorite.

Margie and Sadie
by James Henry Taylor

The two girls were ensconced on a pair of child-sized lawn chairs inside "The Palace," having their tea. It was real tea, taken from a bottle in the refrigerator and allowed to warm up to room temperature.

Margie was about five and a half; she tried to maintain proper posture in her little chair, but had a child's natural tendency to slump, and to swing one leg when she wasn't thinking about it. Sadie was quite a bit smaller than her friend, and remained very stiff in her seat, with her left arm slightly raised; her age was perhaps a matter of academic debate, since she had come from Walmart.

The palace itself was a cardboard construction, really intended for indoor use, but since the National Weather Service had predicted clear skies for several days in a row, her father had carried it out and set it near the young oak tree. He had painted the outside walls a soft blue, added white outlines around the window holes, and used a dull black for the roof. The girl had decorated the interior with "paintings" from her coloring book, an old pink bathroom rug, a child's play table, and of course the folding chairs.

It goes without saying that a child of Margie's age had no

business having a book of matches or a candle. Nevertheless, she'd managed to obtain one of each. She was clever, and after having observed more than once how her parents used them, she only wasted four matches before getting the candle to light. It was then set on the inverted lid of a peanut butter jar as centerpiece for the table.

Margie took occasional sips of her tea from her plastic teacup and chatted away in what she imagined was a royal fashion. Sadie did not, except in Margie's mind.

The girl's mother, Kait, called from the house: "Margie, lunch is ready."

Margie set down her cup: "Excuse me, won't you? I'll be back soon." She trotted across the yard on stout little legs, went directly into the kitchen through the back door, and seated herself at the table. Halfway through a plate of leftover macaroni and cheese with tuna, a commotion from behind the house caught her attention.

The backyard neighbor was shouting for aid as she sprayed down the burning palace with a garden hose. Margie's mother ran outside and grabbed their own hose, shooting water from a pistol-grip nozzle as she dashed across the grass; the girl herself followed close behind, even though her mother kept telling her to keep back. It was only a couple of minutes before the place had been reduced to a sodden, blackened mess draped over the aluminum frames of the table and chairs.

"Sadie," Margie cried out, her girlish fists pressed together against her chest as she rocked from foot to foot. She turned to her mother. "Where's Sadie?"

"I don't know, honey." Kait picked up a stick that was lying in the yard and began peeling away the half-burnt and waterlogged cardboard. When she removed the section covering Sadie's chair, they found the remains of the doll beneath it, naked except for its shoes and socks, the face and body scorched and collapsed inward.

"Sadie! Sadie!"

Margie's mother dropped the hose and held her back with one hand, testing the temperature of the doll with the other. It was cool enough, so she picked it up and gazed at it sadly. "Oh I'm sorry, honey." She hugged her daughter with her free arm.

Margie was trying to hold back tears; a few slipped down her face anyway. "Can't we fix her?"

"I'm sorry but, no ... no, there's nothing we can do. We were too late." She hugged her daughter again and turned her own face to their neighbor. "Thanks, Nora. Did you see how it happened?"

"No, I just happened to look out and I saw it burning. I was so scared that Margie was in there."

"No, thank God."

Nora turned her eyes to the girl. "I'm sorry Margie. I wish I'd got here quicker."

Not knowing what to say, Margie gave a little nod. Her mother gently turned her toward the house, said, "Thanks again, Nora," and started them toward the back door.

"What's going to happen to Sadie?"

"Well ... what do you think we should do?"

Margie remained quiet until they had nearly reached the house. "Maybe we should give her a funeral."

Margie's mother couldn't suppress an affectionate smile. "I think that's a good idea, honey. Where should we do it?"

Margie thought a little more. "Maybe in the garden?"

"Well ..."

Margie's face was partly toward the sun; she squinted

upward at her mother expectantly.

The look made Kait relent. "Yes, I think we can find some space there."

"What will we bury her in?"

"Let's see if we can find a nice box, maybe in your closet."

When they reached Margie's room, Kait pushed the sliding closet door aside. "Do you want to hold Sadie while I look?"

Margie hugged the doll to her chest, but she scanned the possibilities on the shelf and floor. Although Sadie wasn't very tall, the few shoeboxes were far too small, and the brightly colored containers that had held toys did not seem proper, so next they tried the parents' room. Kait took down a dark gray box that held two seldom-worn black pumps. After she placed the shoes with several other pairs on her half of the closet floor, she fluffed up the tissue paper the pumps had been wrapped in, looking thoughtful. Finally, she spoke.

"I have some nice pieces of cloth that we can cover her with." She took her daughter's hand, and they went down the stairs into the finished basement, to the closet where the Christmas things were kept. Kait found the bag that held remainders used for wrapping special gifts, and placed the pieces one at a time on the coffee table in front of the well-worn couch. Margie chose a medium-blue one with gold filigreed stars printed on it; it looked old-fashioned and serious, and somewhat royal.

Margie's mother set the box on the coffee table and reached out to her gently. The girl hesitated a moment or two, then handed Sadie over. After Kait had settled the doll on the bed of tissue paper, Margie covered Sadie with the starry cloth. She tucked it over the doll's body, but left the ruined face exposed. She put one brief kiss on the forehead before Kait placed the lid on the shoebox.

The two went out through the back door to the small patch of flowers by the corner of the house. It was divided into two rectangles, one each of chrysanthemums and of zinnias in multiple colors, with a narrow aisle of bare soil between them. Kait set the coffin on the ground and told her daughter to wait while she got a shovel from the garage. Returning with a small garden trowel, she got on her knees and began digging a little grave in the space separating the beds, where the plants would partly shade it from the sun. In a few minutes, there was a fairly neat rectangular hole about ten inches deep. Kait lowered the box carefully to the bottom, then turned to her daughter. "Now we have to cover it up."

"I know."

"Do you want me to wait a little? Is there anything you want to say?"

Margie was silent for half a minute as she peered into the hole, then said wistfully, "Goodbye, Sadie."

Kait picked up a trowelful of dirt and spread it lightly onto the lid of the box. One scoop followed another until the little grave was filled, then a few more were added to make a mound about an inch high. When Kait had smoothed everything softly with the trowel, the two of them went inside.

Later investigation led to a restrained scolding from her father, a shamed and tearful repentance, and being sent to bed with no after-dinner cartoons.

Margie awoke around two o'clock in the morning. A small voice had been calling her name. She opened her eyes, and there was Sadie, hovering above the foot of Margie's bed. The doll looked almost like her old self, with beige skin and black hair, yet somehow paler, and ripply, with a luminous outline.

"You came back!" Margie whispered, loudly.

Although the doll's lips weren't able to move, she said, *"Yes, I wanted to see you again."*

The voice was in Margie's head—as it always had been—yet somehow it sounded different than before, and she didn't know what Sadie would say before it was said. Suddenly, she couldn't look at her friend, so she turned her eyes down toward the pale blue coverlet. "I'm sorry, I didn't mean to burn you up."

Sadie's tone said that if she could have, she would have smiled. *"I know you didn't do it on purpose. But now you see why little girls shouldn't play with matches."*

A short silence followed. Margie asked, with her eyes still averted, "Did it ... hurt?"

Sadie seemed to ponder before replying, *"Not the way you mean."* She hesitated again. *"Only when I knew it was too late ... it hurt, because ... I knew I wouldn't be here with you anymore."*

Margie quickly looked up. "Can't you stay?"

Sadie shook her doll's head slowly. *"Even if I could, we couldn't play the same way we did before. I could only visit you like this, late at night, when no one else was around."*

"Pleeease?"

"I'm sorry, Margie, but I have no choice. I have to move on."

"Why?"

Sadie paused. *"I can't really explain."*

"But where?"

"I don't really know where I'm going. Only I feel it, that I'm going somewhere."

Margie was quiet for a while before she asked, "Will I go there too ... when ...?"

"I don't know. Maybe."

"Will you ever come back?"

"I don't think so. I don't know why I'm not already gone. It could be because I still had something else to do. Maybe to let you know that I don't blame you."

Soft footsteps approached from Margie's parents' room.

"I'll miss you."

The image of Sadie quickly faded.

Kait quietly pushed the door open, enough so she could peek inside. Margie was still sitting up, staring at where Sadie had been.

"Margie, honey, are you alright?"

"Yes, I'm alright."

"I thought I heard you talking to someone. Were you dreaming?"

"I … I don't know. I thought I saw Sadie."

"Sadie?" Kait sat softly on the edge of the bed. "I know you miss her, honey. But it must have been a dream."

"Are you sure?"

"I think it must have been, Margie."

"But you're not sure?"

Kait nodded gently. "Yes, Margie, I'm sure." She gave Margie's head a caress, and said, "It's time for sleep, now," then added, "Do you want to sleep with us tonight?"

"No, I'm alright." Margie eased herself back and let her mother arrange and smooth the coverlet.

Kait touched her forehead to her daughter's, and followed the touch with a kiss. "Sweet dreams." Then she slipped out the door, leaving it ajar, and padded back down the hallway.

As Margie lay with her eyes shut, wondering if Sadie's visit had really been a dream, a small voice whispered in her ear.

Margie and Sadie

"And thank you for choosing me such a pretty place."
    And Margie smiled a little smile.

Author's Comments:

It took a while for me to choose the "species" for this piece. Almost all ghosts in the stories and movies I know about are ghosts of people, so I wanted something different. An animal? That had been done before, too. (Heck, I'd already used it myself.) A microscopic organism? (Let's drop this line of inquiry.) What about a plant, then: say, a tree? I'd seen possessed trees before in movies—demonic trees, *à la* "Poltergeist"— but the ghost of a tree? Would the main character appear as an otherworldly stump? (I don't know…) The ghost of some flowers? The scent could linger… OK, how about a rock, the ghost of a rock? (Sounds a bit limited.) Finally, I hit on the ghost of a character that straddles the line between the living and the never-having-lived. (And while I'm probably not the first to make this specific choice, at least it isn't too common.)

Night Guardian
by Chanda K. Zimmerman

He awoke, ears twitching. It was the sound that had roused him from his midnight nap. He knew that sound, knew it was time. He stretched his long, black legs, extending every claw, arcing the long tail, and yawning to expose his rather impressive fangs. A moment, and then everything recoiled into perfect symmetry of muscle, bone and reflex. He rose, and began to pad softly through the dark house, pupils growing round to capture every little bit of faint light and more, observing things that no human could ever see.

He patrolled through the familiar rooms of the old Victorian house he now shared with his mistress, asleep on the upper floor with the dog, a rather sociable but not terribly bright, shaggy, elderly little thing of mixed heritage—who was, no doubt, sleeping the sleep of the almost dead, oblivious to the sound. Just as well, given the circumstances.

He knew where the sound was coming from. Even if his ears, sharp enough to identify the exact spot where a mouse wandered inside the walls, or a spider walked along the window sash, had not instantly targeted the location, he knew where it came from because it was not the first time he'd risen to respond.

He found her in the old conservatory, where Mistress

kept her antique baby grand piano and had converted the room into a library filled with tall bookcases and stacks and stacks of books and other documents. It had a nice, homey, messy feel to it. And there, sitting in an old wooden chair with a tall back that faced the small window seat overlooking the garden, was the source of the sound.

He could see her, plain as day, although he knew that to living humans—with their rather dull senses and fixation on the present world—she was ethereal, vague and barely formed. She was weeping again, a deep, endless, and disconcerting sound even to him. He sat down for a moment, wrapping his tail tightly around his feet, watching her and wondering once again what prompted all this misery, this far more than sorrow, this seemingly eternal despair.

He had heard it from time to time since coming to live with his mistress almost a year ago. Some of the other felines, plump, spoiled, but on the whole a decent bunch, sought out refuges of peace and quiet on the upper floors, even the rather stuffy and odd third floor, or in any of the many hiding places to be found in this old, rather decaying brick mansion … far away from this pitiful apparition and her inconsolable grief. He understood their withdrawal. It was hard to bear another's pain, especially when you couldn't do anything to help.

But he had decided some time ago that even though there was a veil between them, an endless chasm of time and space, he could try. He knew Mistress was partly aware of the other denizens of the house, those misty apparitions that sometimes flickered in the corner of her sight, or left a chilling aura in a room, or simply made their presence known in other not-so-subtle ways. They distressed her, worried her that they had no peace … but she was too kindhearted to even seek a way to clear the house of its other presences. After all, as she'd told him many times when stroking him on her lap, they had been here long before she bought the old place, so what gave her the right to kick them out?

But they frightened her nonetheless. He'd felt the flutter of her pulse when a chill gloom descended on a room, or a swirl of mist passed across one of the wide, arched doorways in the twilight of a winter's day. She kept more lights on than necessary, often had a radio on in various rooms, grateful for the sound of disembodied voices whose origin at least she knew and could control.

He wanted to tell her it was all right, that none of them was harmful—and if they had been, she had him now to protect her, to bridge the chasm, to warn them to be respectful and gracious in their shared existence.

And when occasionally they grew restless … when something fell that should not have fallen, or a picture straightened an hour ago was suddenly cockeyed on the wall … when something rattled upstairs, or a knock was heard in the kitchen or from the cellar … or an unfelt breeze scattered papers on the floor … his mistress grew increasingly uneasy, even afraid, although she wouldn't admit it even to herself. She wasn't young anymore, although she seemed to the world to be solid and steady enough. But he knew, they all knew, that she was getting on in years. They could smell the steady march of time, the underlying health issues she knew about and took medicine for, and some she didn't, and the occasional, unexpected shift in the beats of her too kind heart.

Then he roused the other cats, and together they took up the challenge to ensure that she could rest easy. They would dash through the house, making noise, scattering papers, brushing pictures large and small upon the walls with their flying tails, and racing along precipitously staged displays of "pretties"—antique glass vases, delicate figurines, etc.—and even occasionally, audaciously, knocking a cup or other object to the floor and risking a scolding. That last was, of course, mere performance art: like all their kind, they could have threaded a perfect path through even the most intricate display of delicate china without moving anything, if they so desired.

But their wild-eyed, kitten antics, wrestling with rugs and tossing ridiculous fabric mice into the air with crazy abandon, served its purpose. Mistress would begin to smile, then laugh, her fears of ghosts and other things laid to rest in the sweet release of pure joy in her little tribe.

But now, there was another fearful heart to lay to rest, at least for tonight. He rose, and approached the figure in the chair, a young woman, her hair unbound and hanging down to the bustline of her long dress from another time. She was hunched and crying pitifully into her hands. He could not climb on her lap as he did the mistress's, or even touch her without his paw passing right through her faint and feeble form, existing in some other dimension. But he did what he could.

He lay down, and curled up at her feet, at the very tip of little toes in the soft antique house slippers with their satin bows. Turning himself slightly to reveal his face and throat, his paws held close to his chest in happiness as he channeled from memories of sunny afternoons and enticing Christmas trees with their dangling ornaments … he began to purr. Soft at first, then more loudly, until he fell into the rhythm, and it became a natural, throaty sound that rose to the weeping woman above him, crossing all barriers of time and space.

It took a little while, but eventually the weeping began to

slow to snuffles and then to a delicate, poised silence. He kept purring, not daring to open his eyes, and not really inclined to do so anyway since the purring had put him in a state of simple, peaceful bliss. Finally, he heard it, what he'd been waiting for—the long, soft sigh as she settled, calm now. He heard the clock ticking faintly in the main parlor far to the front of the house, and kept *purring, purring, purring*, steady as a little engine and calming as a warm cup of tea, a stroke of a loving hand against a cheek or hair, a memory that led a lost heart back to a warm place.

After several minutes, he realized he didn't feel the presence of her shoes behind his back, didn't feel the cool aura of her form on the chair. All seemed still in the conservatory … until he heard a single note from the piano, a delicate, tiny sound more like a pluck of a string than a touch upon an ivory key that flitted away like a memory. Then she was gone.

He slowed his purring—letting himself come back to the present, to the reality of the old house with its smells and natural creaks of old wood, mice in the walls, and spiders hunting outside the front door and the back one in the kitchen. He rolled over, sat up, and took a quick bath to ground himself again.

Satisfied, he padded back through the old house to the warmer spot on the cushiony sofa in the side parlor, where they all watched television most nights with the mistress, and shared the communal love that was such a gift after his first few years as a youngster in a big, scary world, alone in the dark with all the hunters of the night and the dangers of the day … until he had been found, rescued, and adopted. He felt a strong sense of satisfaction from sharing what he could to ease another's pain in gratitude for those who had eased his own

…and hoped it would be a few days before another one of the house's old residents needed comforting.

He paused as he passed the stairs, considering just for a moment whether to join the elderly dog on Mistress's bed. Then he padded on to the side parlor and the soft sofa, ears twitching as he heard the tiny little chime of the mantle clock in the front parlor strike 4 a.m.

Author's Comments:

I live with eight cats, sometimes more, and have always had a cat around the house since I was a wee child, along with dogs, etc. One thing I like about cats—and something my cat-loving friends share—is a belief that cats, like most animals, can see the spirit world. Cats also provide a reassuring presence in a house: any noise heard during the night can be easily attributed to them nosing about! A friend had recently lost her beloved black cat, and I immediately thought of him as the main character, and I know most of my animals are very sensitive to my emotions, especially depression. So, it simply seemed natural for a cat to interact with a ghost. The story came to me in a moment of routine "meditation" (the kind that happens as you move about the world), and I wrote it quickly in one sitting because it felt so clear and natural.

About the Authors

John Hanford retired from the United States Army in 1991. He then attended Kansas State University, acquiring a degree in English and special education from Kansas State University. He worked in education until 2009 when he retired from his position as Director of Special Education of Grain Valley Missouri School District. He writes poetry, fiction, and non-fiction—his short-story, "A Boy," was a  runner-up for the David Baker Award, University of Central Missouri, 2014. John continues to study writing and other areas of interest. He is an avid photographer, landscaper, and traveler.

Chuck Hocter has retired three times and failed miserably at it three times. He spent 20 years in the USAF, 19 years in a battery factory and 9 months as Chief Dust Bunny Herder in a lint factory. Now he works for a wonderful boss who also happens to be his lovely wife of 43 years, Theresa. His interests are limited to reading, writing, riding motorcycles, and doing whatever the boss says. He is a graduate of  the University of Central Missouri with a degree in Creative Writing. He has published a novel—M.O.B. (Mean Old Bastard), available on Amazon. He has started at least six other novels, none of which will be ready for publication anytime soon. Two of his short stories have appeared in anthologies published by Literary Lab. At present, most of his time is taken up by caring for his massive F-350 named BYGGIE, his Ranger LI'L RED, his two motorcycles (unnamed), his dog Butch, and his cat Baby, whose real name is Shiva, The Destroyer. Oh, yeah, and the BOSS.

R.M. Kinder is a retired professor of English (Creative Writing), a musician, and an amateur naturalist. Her most recent publications are *A Common Person and Other Stories* (Richard Sullivan Short Fiction Award, 2021 University of Notre Dame Press) and *A Cat for All Seasons*, an animal-fiction novel released for the Christmas holiday. For more publication and biographical details, please visit her website at rmkinder.net. Her blog is Digressions.

James Henry Taylor's publications include three collections of short fiction—*Sleeping Life and Other Stories* (Sweetgum Press 2017), *Everyday Wonder, or The Quick Brown Fox Jumps Over the Lazy Dog* (Sweetgum Press 2010), and *Honeysuckle and Other Stories* (Cave Hollow Press 2002)—as well as the novel *Convenience Store Vampire* (a Barnes & Noble Nook book 2011), and papers in scientific journals such as *Physical Review B, Il Nuovo Cimento,* and *Journal of Statistical Mechanics: Theory and Experiment.* He has a B.S. in Physics from Rensselaer Polytechnic Institute and a Ph.D from University of Rhode Island.

Chanda K. Zimmerman's credits include a short story listed in *The Year's Best Horror and Fantasy for 2006*, a children's non-fiction book, and several documentary films, as well as numerous business presentations and speeches. Her greatest delight when not writing is caring for her eight cats. To learn more, visit her website/blog at chandakzimmerman.com. 
Chanda has an M.F.A. in Professional Writing from the University of Southern California and a B.A. in TV/Film Production and Sociology from Trinity University (TX).

www.ingramcontent.com/pod-product-compliance
Lightning Source LLC
Chambersburg PA
CBHW021655110726
47902CB00007B/1943